Murder
at
The Belly Up

A NOVEL BY T.J. CAHILL

ISBN 1461096081
EAN-139781461096085

ACKNOWLEDGEMENTS

As always, I have to thank Jeffery Etter in a big way for making my manuscript look like a book. This is our third collaboration and every time he puts his creative designs to work I thank God that he is as talented as he is. I am looking forward to another thirty collaborations with him. None better.

Agatha Christie is the very best at this genre and I just wanted, for a brief moment, to see what it would be like to stand in her shadow. It's a nice feeling. I think I'll try it again!

Eileen Rosenberger is the best friend anyone can have. She's always there for me with an encouraging word (and she knows when I need them the most!). She's kind, thoughtful, beautiful, intelligent, funny and very creative in her own right. She makes me want to be a better man, so I keep trying.

The gang at A.R's did more for me this past year than they know. What a crowd! I could not have written this novel without them. They turned Happy Hour into the happiest hours.

DEDICATION

My beloved Ireland is in a bad way right now. A bit tattered around the edges as they say – sort of like good 'ol Mugsy at the beginning of this story. Once you finish this novel, you'll see how the regal Irish breed successfully weathers a bad time. Without stretching the analogy too much, I know the same will happen for everyone in Ireland. So, this book is dedicated to them and their big comeback!

Chapter One

From the outside, it looked fairly non-descript. It was undistinguishable from the other hundred or so bars in Belleva County. Oh, it had the usual bar-type advertisements in the front window....2 for 1 Happy Hour, big screen t.v. for the major sports events, special "party nights" for St. Paddy's Day, Halloween and so on. But whether The Belly Up was *really* a sports bar was often left up to booze-infused debates. Once in a while a good crowd would gather inside for a big NFL football game but usually by half-time, somebody with two or three more beers in them than sobriety allowed would start yelling for the bartender to put some Johnny Cash music on the jukebox.

The Belly Up was a bar.....plain and simple. People went in there to get half a load on. It wasn't actually as dingy as a lot of "all drunks welcome" holes-in-the wall are. There were certainly a lot worse looking places in Belleva County. But there was only one Belly Up. Some people had been going there for years. Some were new to the place. Some were pretty old and some were not so old. Most of the time, everybody was welcome. Everybody, except one: Larry Lutursky

Larry Lutursky was a seventy-eight year old major pain in the ass. He started drinking at The Belly Up when he was sixteen years old. He snuck in at night after Pasquale, the owner, went home and Mickey O'D tended bar. Mickey let anybody in if they had the dough to buy a drink. He figured it was more tips for him and his brother, Brian, was the beat cop who always turned a blind eye when his little brother was behind the bar. So Larry was a flat out alkie by the time he was eighteen. The past six decades of pouring beer and shots of Jack Daniels down his throat didn't do a thing to improve his rotten disposition. The only thing different now was that Peitro, Pasquale's youngest son, was running the bar.

Back in those early days, Mickey always felt a bit sorry for Larry. Well, the truth is he felt "half-sorry" for him. Larry was half Irish and half Hungarian. It was the Hungarian half that Mickey O'D felt sorry for. "He ain't never going to amount to nothin' – not with that lousy Hungarian heart of his" Mickey would always tell his brother, Officer O'Donnell. Brian always readily agreed. "He's eighteen years old and he ain't never had a steady job. He should try walkin' the beat sometime." Brian's suggestion brought pales of Irish laughter from his bartender brother. "He'd never get on the force!! Besides, would you want a boyo like him carryin' a loaded gun?" Brian looked down at the far end of the bar – the dark end – and just shook his head. "Look at him. Eighteen years old and stinkin' drunk before the stroke of midnight. He's a disgrace to the Irish."

"The Irish half is the only reason I been lettin' him in this bar for two years." Mickey nodded with a wink "and it's usually the Hungarian half that that tries to skip out without leavin' me a tip for my troubles!" He slapped his hand on the bar for the telling of the tale "and it's the Hungarian half I don't mind punchin' in the nose!!"

Over the years Larry Lutursky received more than just a few punches in the nose. His bad attitude and drunkenness resulted in him getting a few broken ribs, a couple of concussions and on three separate and different occasions, three broken noses out in the back of the bar. In one fight, he got a serious, deep slash across the right side of his face with somebody's serrated-edged knife. That was back in 1972 and nobody ever knew what it was for and everybody involved in the confrontation was now dead – except for Larry and he never talked about it. And as painfully obvious as the long, deep scar still was on his face all these thirty-nine years later, Larry never talked about it to anybody. In fact, Larry hardly ever talked to anybody about anything. He just sat there at the dark end of the bar and drank his bottled beer and whiskey shots. But it was clear that nobody really liked Larry – never did.

Over the sixty-two years that he'd been coming into The Belly Up, that never changed.

The Belly Up opened up at Noon every day and stayed open until 4:00 am. It wasn't unusual at all to see two or three guys waiting in line for Patti-cake, the daytime bartender, to unlock the door. "Patti-cake" was just her nickname. Her real name was Helenka Stropoudanolupolkis. But since none of the drunks could actually pronounce her full name, they called her Patti-cake because she was so pretty. She was everything a female daytime bartender should be. Cute, buxom, sassy and savvy as hell. Patti-cake was "sweet as pie and tough as leather" as the old song goes. At thirty-six years old, bartending was what she knew and she was real good at her job. She could charm the skin off a snake and "the money out of our pockets" as one of her regulars, Barry the Gambler, always liked to announce. If Barry wasn't gambling, he was making announcements about all the goings on in Belleva County. Some of his news was not always reliable, but it was always a big announcement. He liked to call attention to himself that way.

Patti-cake kept a close eye on Larry. In the five years that she had been tending bar at The Belly Up, Larry had hardly ever said anything except "Good Morning" to her. He never said "Good-Bye", though. He just got up and left. But she watched him like a hawk. She knew about his reputation but always told Peitro that "he never causes any trouble on my shifts. He never even leers at me!" she said with a laugh. Half the old timers who came in to The Belly Up in the daytime came into leer at Patti-cake and she knew it. Hers was the kind of classic female figure that old timers leered at. "Look but don't touch" was the order of the day and probably the story of their lives. Leerers are generally made that way. But everyone was entitled to look.

And she knew what everyone's "usual" was, too. One of her claims to fame was that if you were new to the bar, she'd actually make up one for you.

Muldoon Frickey walked into The Belly Up one afternoon and ordered a bottle of Sam Adams and Patti-cake just looked at him. He looked back at her and repeated "A bottle of Sam Adams, if you have it, please."

"You new here?" she asked bending ever so suggestively over the bar. He nodded wondering what it was going to take to get a simple bottle of cold beer.

"Ok." she smiled "*Your* 'usual' is going to be a Bombay Sapphire gin martini – VERY dry – straight up with a couple of olives!!" Muldoon looked at her like she was from the moon.

"Just a cold bottle of Sam – that'll do it for me." he replied as patiently as he could

After some bantering and easy bickering back and forth, Muldoon wound up with his cold beer – poured into a martini glass! And Patti-cake laughed that enchanting Melina Mercouri-laugh of hers while she poured. Barry the Gambler was right, she could charm the skin off a snake and the money right out of your pocket.

Muldoon was impressed.

Impressed enough to, in time, become a "sort-of" regular at
The Belly Up. He could not meet the standard of being a real
regular, which meant you had to be at the bar every day for hours
on end. That kind of a thing is a real job killer and Muldoon had
a job, after all. It was his second job – or to be more exact – it was
his second career. He was retired from the police force after putting in his minimum twenty years and mustered out at the ripe old
age of thirty-eight. He never made detective because he couldn't
pass the test. It wasn't that he wasn't smart enough. He was just
a very bad test taker. Muldoon had plenty of smarts. But what
made him such a good cop was that he had "street smarts" flowing
out his ears.

With twenty years of savings and a nice pension to rely on,
Muldoon bummed around the world for two years after he left the
force. He always wanted to travel but never found the time while
wearing a badge.

"A cop is always a cop" his old man told him before he went
into the Police Academy "don't forget that. There ain't no down
time." Muldoon's father was one to know. He put twenty-five
years in on the force before he was shot down in the dead of night
He was off-duty and tried to abort a robbery in progress at a
bodega. The robber turned quickly and fired two shots from a .45
straight through Officer Frickey's heart. BAM! BAM! Dead on
the spot. Nobody was ever caught.

So after his own retirement, Muldoon went all the places
he ever wanted to go. He spent weeks after leisurely weeks in
London, Paris, Berlin, Barcelona and Rome. Then it was off to
Athens, Istanbul and a month and a half in Moscow. He broke
his own rule about the tediousness of sunbathing and spent three
weeks enjoying the sun and sand in Crete. But for him nothing

compared to seeing the Taj Mahal in India and the Great Wall of China. Tokyo was a bust as was Hawaii, he thought. He recalled with great fondness his three-month long shack-up with Mataki, his island honey on Borneo which made him skip his planned visit to New Zealand. He really wished he would have seen New Zealand but Mataki was way too beautiful to resist.

Before he went home he decided to fly to Los Angles to line up with all the other crazy movie fans at the 82nd Annual Academy Awards. After twenty years on the force in the big city, he really hated crowds. But, he wanted to see if he might be able to get Clint Eastwood's autograph. He did. Even shook his hand. "Better than a week of nights with Mataki." he thought as he tucked the precious autograph away in his tattered paperback copy of "War and Peace". It was the only book he brought along with him on his travels. It took him two years to read it.

Two suitcases and two years later, Muldoon Frickey was heading home to a new life. He wanted some peace and quiet so he picked a nice log cabin on Frettyman Lake in Belleva County. It was about four miles from The Belly Up and just over a half a mile away from his new rented office space that had a nice sign outside - Muldoon Frickey: Private Investigator. He always loved coming up to Frettyman Lake as a kid with his father on fishing vacations. It was just far enough away from the big city. And now it was just far enough away to leave his old job and his old life behind.

He was driving back to the lake from the local post office when he felt a raging thirst for a beer that enticed him into The Belly Up that very first day….when he learned that his "usual" was going to be a dry martini.

But it was fate that brought him right inside to lay his eyes on the craggy, scar-faced Larry Lutursky for the very first time.

Muldoon Frickey, the forty-year old retired single cop, devil-may-care world traveler, and now a self-employed licensed private detective had just bellied up to the bar for the case of his life.

All for the price of a cold beer in a martini glass and the come-hither laughter of a Greek barmaid.

Chapter Two

Muldoon was still half asleep in bed when he heard the car tires run slowly over the gravel in his driveway. He looked out the bedroom window and saw a police car come to a halt just before the steps leading to the front porch.

"Muldoon Frickey!! Muldoon Frickey are you in there?" the cop shouted. "Muldoon Frickey – you are under arrest!!!! Come out with your hands up!"

Muldoon put his glasses on and slowly pulled the curtain back from the window with his left hand. He could hardly believe his eyes. With his right hand he lifted up the window and stuck his head out and shouted back "It wasn't me copper!! Besides she said she was eighteen!!"

As he bounded down the stairs, the officer approached the front screen door and hit it with a few good knocks. "Get out of bed you lazy ass and make me some coffee! It's 9:00 am – what are you still doing in bed?"

Muldoon opened the front door and extended his hand for a hearty handshake. "It's Saturday, you moron. Besides, how the hell did you ever find me here?" he asked.

The cop was Peter Branderford – Muldoon's partner for three years.

"I'm the Chief of Police up here now! I got the job right after you went off to travel to God only knows where."

"You are the Chief!!" replied Muldoon "What? --- Nobody else applied for the job?" he added jokingly.

"Who cares? I had seventeen years on the force in the big city and had enough of the scumbags but not enough time in to retire. So, this gig came up and I took it. Jesus, it's like being the sheriff of Mayberry for Christ's sake compared to what we saw together."

Muldoon walked his former partner through the living room and into the large kitchen in the back of the house. Peter took one look around and whistled that kind of whistle that guys do when they are fairly amazed at what they see. "Man…what a view of the lake you have here."

"I think I got a bit of the old Irish luck when I bought this place."

"Typical." said Peter with a wry note in his reply.

"Not that I don't deserve it, mind you!" said Muldoon "I worked mighty hard for twenty years and this place reminds me of the times I spent fishing up here with my father."

Peter knew all about how the senior Officer Frickey died and never talked about him – even when the junior Officer Frickey did. He just let it slide on by and often changed the subject. "How's your mother?" he said.

"Same old, same old" was the terse reply "I don't see much of her and hear even less. It's better that way."

The momentary awkward silence found Muldoon pouring too much coffee and grabbing a paper towel to wipe up the mess.

"Same old Muldoon" laughed Peter "clean and neat as a pin and orderly to a fault."

He thanked him for the cup of coffee and took a seat at the round kitchen table.

Muldoon rebounded from his unpleasant familial reflection

with a real question for his former partner. "So how the hell *did* you find me way out here?"

"Well, all the new licenses for whatever professions are filed with the Chamber of Commerce and they send a copy over to my office. I was working late last night and came across your P.I. license. I thought I was seeing things. How long have you been back?"

"Oh…I'd say just a little over five months."

"You've been up here on the lake for five months?!"

"No…no…it took me a month to find this place and then after I made an offer…I guess it was two months to close on the property and then a month or so to get it all furnished….I guess I've been actually living here for about a month….maybe a little less."

"I guess you don't get into town much. You work from home?"

"Nope" replied Muldoon "never did like that notion much – "working from home" – too easy to lay around and watch old movies on t.v. all day. No….I need to get up and go to an office so I rented a place about a half a mile down the road. Just a small place to hang out my shingle."

"You and your old movies! You've probably seen every old movie ever made."

"Some of them several times over!

"Who are you renting from"?

"His name is Butterman….George Butterman…..I think he's a local guy…know him?"

"Sure do." said Peter "he owns about half the town and a good chunk of other real estate in Belleva County. He's a good man to know as long as you're on his good side."

"Hmmmm…..I'll try to remember that." Muldoon grabbed his coffee mug and joined Peter at the table. "So….how's married life treating you?"

"Strained as always." Peter paused for a moment while Muldoon waited for what he was pretty sure was coming. "Jennie's not with me up here.....I mean she comes up every now and again but she doesn't like it up here and says the schools are inferior..... no good for the kids. I mean what does she know?"

"She's their mother.....she might have some insight into it."

"Bullshit" snapped Peter "we both know our kids are morons. 'Sesame Street' was too much for them. She spoiled them rotten. No discipline whatsoever and now they are morons."

"They're teenagers, for Christ's sake!"

"Same thing." added Peter.

"By the look of your left hand, I'd say things have deteriorated somewhat."

"Hmmm?" Muldoon pointed to Peter's hand. "No wedding ring, my man."

"Oh....that. Yeah well, I find it a deterrent socially speaking."

Muldoon just laughed at the thought of his old partner out on the dating scene. He reached for Peter's coffee mug. "How about a refill?"

"Can't. But thanks anyway. I have to be getting back into town. I just thought I'd roll a bit of the Welcome Wagon out for you."

"I appreciate it, Peter. It's good to see you again."

They both walked out to Peter's squad car. Peter looked around and said "You sure have a nice piece of property out here. A real slice of heaven." Muldoon nodded.

"What are you going to do now for the rest of this beautiful day now that I got you out of bed early on a Saturday?!"

"Oh...I don't know. I was thinking of going over to the pound and rescuing a dog. I need some company out here. Come back and maybe watch an old movie."

"What – 'Play Misty for Me' for the 50th time!!"

Muldoon just smiled. "Something like that."

"Well, don't be a stranger." said Peter as he hopped into the driver's seat.

Muldoon waved as he drove away and thought to himself "That guy is not happy – definitely not happy."

He turned to walk back into the house and said aloud "A dog – now *that's* a great idea!!"

Chapter Three

On his way into the dog pound, Muldoon made a quick stop by his office and smiled when he saw his shingle hanging outside. "Yeah - this is going to suit me just fine" he mused. "I like the feel of it."

When he got inside he smiled again at the fax tray which had a small pile of faxes in it. "Yep! Muldoon Frickey: Private Investigator – open for business!" he shouted. The faxes were just what he was expecting – just not so many of them right off the bat.

One of his old pals on the force, Gerry Dowling, was also retired and now working for a private security firm in the big city. He promised to send Muldoon some overflow business on simple stuff like credit and background checks. Easy as pie to do and a good way to get his business jump started. He quickly looked over the dozen or so faxes and did not notice anything suspicious so he laid them on his desk. "I can knock most of them off on Monday, no problem" he said "then I'll give 'ol Ger a ring and thank him. But for now I am off to see what the pound has in the line of a new best friend for me."

Relaxed, showered, shaved and a belly full of his own best pancakes, Muldoon was enjoying a slow drive into town. It was the first time he truly noticed and admired the rolling countryside on either side of the two-lane road. It was pretty country and Muldoon was getting a homey feeling. He briefly thought of his old partner, Peter Branderford. "I can't blame Pete for wanting to live up here. It sure beats the big city. But that whole marriage set-up of his is for the birds."

Truth was, anybody's marriage set-up to Muldoon was for the birds. He was just not the marrying kind – at all. He could go on all night about the pros of women and the cons of marriage. He came close one time while he was a rookie on the force and then thought better of the whole deal. He was never really engaged but when his live-in girlfriend started to buy "Bride's Magazine", Muldoon started to get nervous. She found the magazines in the garbage one day and promptly moved out. And Muldoon moved on. "No clipped wings for Officer Frickey's boy!!" was his mantra. He liked it that way and that's the way it was going to stay.

He caught all the red lights as soon as he pulled onto Main Street. Normally just a little impatient, he was in no hurry this afternoon and the stop-and-go traffic all along the street gave him a good chance to do some people watching through the front windshield of his Ford pick-up truck – a red F-150 Raptor SVT he picked up at a sheriff's sale in the big city a week after he bought his cabin.

There was a good bit of foot traffic for a small town on nice Saturday. People were coming and going, getting errands and chores done. There was a steady flow of shoppers in and out of the supermarket and the Rite-Aid. He could tell that there were already customers seated at a lot of the tables at the Italian restaurant on the corner. Nobody was in the Chinese restaurant just yet but there was a line outside the German Meat Market. The sidewalk sandwich board outside their door advertised home-made franks and bratwurst and a special on smoked pork chops. Muldoon made a mental note of that. The bodega in the middle of the next block reminded him too much of how his father died so he ignored it and started to look more carefully for the dog pound. He glanced again at the address he wrote down on his yellow pad and compared it against the address of the German Meat Market. It looked like the pound might be about a block away or so. Sure enough, when Muldoon began to focus on the addresses he could figure out that the pound was at the end of the second block down the street.

Coincidentally, it was three doors down from The Belly Up – something he did not notice the first day he walked in there. Stuck at another red light, he was able to peer in the open door and see that there were already five or six customers seated at the bar. Muldoon wondered if Patti-cake worked on Saturdays. "Maybe I'll stop in for a quick one before I hit the pound." He turned around and drove two blocks back to a parking lot next to the German Meat Market and gave the teenaged attendant the required $3.50 for an hour. "Nice wheels, dude!" the boy exclaimed as Muldoon gave him $10. "You keep an eye on it for me and you can keep the change, got it?"

"Awesome, dude. Awesome!"

On his stroll over to The Belly Up, Muldoon quizzically wondered why everything was always "awesome" and everybody was a "dude" to teenagers. "Maybe Peter is right – maybe they *are* all morons."

He walked into The Belly Up and didn't recognize anybody – not unusual for only his second time in the bar. He was mildly disappointed not to see Patti-cake behind the bar, though.

"What can I do you for?" said the bartender.

"A bottle of Sam Adams – nice and cold."

"You want a glass?"

"Bottle's fine."

The bartender tossed the cardboard coaster advertising the

German Meat Market on the bar and placed the cold bottle of beer right on top of it.

"You're new here aren't you? I've been here every Saturday for two years and I don't recall your face. You look like you are looking for somebody. I can tell these things." He paused for a moment to size Muldoon up. "I'm Teddy, by the way."

Muldoon firmly shook the bartender's hand and replied "Frickey….Muldoon Frickey's my name. I was in here once before – middle of the week and……"

Teddy immediately interrupted him. "And you came in all shaved and showered and looking good hoping that Patti-cake would be here – right?!" Muldoon flushed a little from embarrassment at being so obviously caught.

He tried to recover by telling Teddy that he was really on his way to the dog pound and just stopped in for a cold one.

"And what – you got all cleaned up this morning to take a dog out on a date?" Teddy teased. "No…no, my friend – you came in looking all snappy on a boring Saturday afternoon to feast your eyes on the pretty Patti-cake." They both laughed even though Muldoon knew it was only half-true. "Don't sweat it, man ….she has that effect on guys. Everybody wants some and nobody gets any…..although I'll admit, you look like you might have a shot."

Muldoon was now paying close attention to Teddy.

"What are you – 6'3" – maybe 6'4"? I got an eye for these things – even at distance."

"I'm 6 feet 2 and a half inches in my stocking feet" admitted Muldoon "and I weigh 192 pounds *before* I sit down for a full meal."

"I was going to guess that" answered Teddy "like I said, I got an eye for these things. And you look like you might be in your early to mid -30's – am I right?"

"Dead wrong there, Teddy. I'm 40 on the nose."

Muldoon had always looked a lot younger than he really was. It posed a problem for him when he first joined the police academy at eighteen. When he was a rookie, he still looked like he was fifteen years old. A tough fifteen year old, nonetheless – but in the beginning it was hard for him to get the jaded perps to take him seriously. Except, when he drew his weapon – then *everybody* took Muldoon seriously. He was a dead aim with a gun.

"Well, I'm not very good at guessing ages, anyway.....but height and weight, I'm usually spot on." boasted Teddy as he handed Muldoon another Sam Adams "it's on the house since you beat me at guessing your real age!"

Muldoon still had a thirst for that second beer and accepted it gladly. "Hey, Teddy – here's a chance for you to redeem yourself. Should be easy. How old do you think that geezer is at the end of the bar down there?"

Muldoon was pointing to Larry Lutursky who had just walked in the back entrance to the bar and plopped himself down in his usual seat at the dark end of the bar.

Oh, *him*." said Teddy with noticeable distain "how *ever* old he is, he's probably lived too long. There's a lot of people around here who are surprised he's even still alive,.....I'm surprised somebody didn't put the nasty old bastard out of his misery long ago."

"Geeze…doesn't exactly sound like he's Mr. Popularity. Who is he anyway?" asked Muldoon.

Teddy gave him a brief back story on Larry and quickly ended it with "and he's a shitty tipper, too."

"Hard drinker?" asked Muldoon

"Hard enough" was the answer "for a guy who's pushing eighty years old and has spent most of the last sixty years in varying stages of an alcoholic haze."

"Why do you let him in here?" was Muldoon's next question as he gave Larry a good looking over.

"If I had to throw everybody out of here who had a nasty disposition, I'd be hard pressed for tips."

Teddy excused himself as he walked down to the other end of the bar to give Larry his usual – a shot of Jack Daniels and a cold Budweiser. Larry barely snorted in response to Teddy's *faux* politeness but it was clear that he was returning Muldoon's "good looking over" while Teddy turned his back and walked away. His stare was not lost on Muldoon. "That guy's got a beef the size of Texas." Muldoon mumbled to himself.

"Hey Teddy" one of the other customers shouted "it's too quiet in here – play me some Johnny Cash!!"

"Hey, Carl" Teddy shouted back "play your own Johnny Cash!"

"C'mon Teddy...you know I don't know how to use that new jukebox...press this...press that...I get thirsty just tryin' to figure it out.....how 'bout a little of the Man in Black for your old pal, eh?....here's a five dollar bill."

"Yeah, I'm your 'old pal'alright" said Teddy as he took the fiver and walked over to the juke.

"What kind of music you like, Muldoon?" asked Teddy

"Cash has always been alright with me....why don't you throw in "King of the Road" by Roger Miller...that is, if Carl there won't mind?"

"King of the Road" is OK by me" yelled Carl as he took another big gulp of his third vodka on the rocks. "My name's Carl, buddy....what's yours."

"Muldoon."

Carl took another swig out of his glass. "Hey Michael....let me ask you something OK?"

"It's Muldoon.....not Michael."

"Well, lemme ask you something anyway OK? Who's your favorite actress?"

Muldoon wasn't sure he heard the question correctly. It seemed like an odd sort of question for anybody to ask a stranger – especially in a bar like The Belly Up.

"Well…I'm not really sure, Carl….I'd have to think about it" was the best answer Muldoon could come up with on the spot – because he was almost certain that old Carl would have no idea who Jennifer Lopez was.

"Ya know who mine is?" said Carl pouring the last of the vodka down his throat.

Muldoon turned to Teddy at the juke and shrugged "Surprise me, Carl."

"Mine's Claudette Colbert! Man, what an actress…lemme tell ya!"

Muldoon laughed out loud and decided to lay some old movie triva (that he was so good at) on Carl. "Yeah…she really deserved that 1934 Best Actress Oscar for 'It Happened One Night'…but Carl, don't you think that she should have gotten another one for "The Egg and I"?

"She shoulda had a hundred of 'em!!" protested Carl "what an actress…lemma tell ya!" Teddy walked back behind the bar and gave Muldoon a wink.

"Hey, Teddy…I'm dry here…pour me another will ya?"

"OK, Carl….but you have to knock off that best actress shit…….every time you have three vodkas on the rocks, you start asking everybody the same damn question."

Muldoon egged Carl a little more "Yeah….Claudette was alright in my book, Carl."

"Goddamn right!" he yelped back.

They all had a laugh as the easy strains of Roger Miller's "King of the Road" started to fill the bar.

When the music came on, Larry Lutursky walked out the back door.

Nobody cared. Nobody noticed. Except Muldoon. "There's *definitely* something strange about that guy" he thought quietly as he said so-long to Teddy and Carl...and Carl's recollections of Claudette Colbert.

Chapter Four

Muldoon decided to name his new dog Mugsy. Mugsy was on "death row" in the pound. Most people come in looking for a puppy to save (for their kids), not a full grown dog. And *nobody* ever came through the door and asked if there were any Irish Wolfhounds "on the block", so to speak. As luck would have it (or as Muldoon's *Irish* luck would have it), Mugsy was there in a cage about to be "put down" as they say.

He was skinny and his coat was dirty and thin --- in some spots there was no coat at all. He had horribly spindly legs and his head drooped almost to the floor when he stood up. Muldoon was appalled.

"What happened to this dog?" he asked Kitty, the owner/ manager of the pound.

"This poor animal was abandoned and probably left for dead in the park that's just four blocks from the end of Main Street. Two kids came in one day and told us there was a dead dog in the park – well, believe me they weren't far from wrong. We had to use a stretcher to get him over here because he was too weak to stand or walk.

"How old is he? How long has he been here?" Muldoon wanted to know.

"I reckon he's about two and a half or three years old and he's been here five weeks" replied Kitty "and that's a week longer than we usually keep them here; but it broke my heart to think that he'd have to be put down. The Irish Wolfhound is such a regal breed – they're such beautiful animals that I would start to weep at the notion that we'd have to kill him."

Muldoon shuddered when Kitty uttered the phrase "kill him". He knew in an instant that he would take this dog home with him but he wondered who could have abandon him in such a sorry state. What kind of *human* animal was so low as to treat such a loving animal so wickedly?

"I'll take him" he said to Kitty.

"I have to tell you up front, Mr. Frickey......"

"Call me Muldoon, please."

"OK. But, I have to tell you up front, Muldoon, that we x-rayed this dog after we finally got him in here and there's no doubt in our minds that he was severely beaten. The x-rays showed some cracked ribs."

"Beaten and starved......I hope I never find out who did this to him."

"There's no way of telling....could have been anybody.... could have been from another town and purposely dumped in our park."

"No I.D. tag...no collar...no nothing?"

"Nada" said Kitty. "Oh, there was this one thing....a leather leash that he had around his neck. We had to sedate him so we could cut it off."

"Do you still have it?"

"I don't know" said Kitty "I'll have to ask Frank. He deals with all the old I.D. tags, name plates, collars....that sort of thing. He keeps them in a box in the back."

"Can you check that out for me, Kitty? Is Frank here today?"

"Sure. I'll go talk to him now."

"Thanks. That'll give me and Mugsy here a few minutes to get acquainted" said Muldoon with a smile.

"That's what you are going to call him? --- Mugsy?"

"Yep. He looks like a Mugsy don't you think --- tough old fella."

Muldoon opened the door to Mugsy's cage and crouched down at the entrance. The dog began to whimper at his approach so Muldoon stayed in a crouched position as he extended his hand to gently pet the dog's front paw. Muldoon was taken aback when Mugsy started to shiver. He didn't know if it was from being cold or that he was scared that he was in for another beating.

Whatever it was, Muldoon was determined to let him know that he was safe.

"Don't you worry about a thing now fella – not a single thing. Muldoon's here and you are going to be fit as a fiddle in no time. Don't you worry at all. Why in no time, you'll be running around like you were born in Ireland!"

Muldoon could hear Kitty coming through the door. "We still had it, Muldoon!" she shouted "Frank found it at the bottom of his box." Muldoon raised his hand to stop her from coming any further. "Can you put it in a brown bag for me, Kitty? Double bag it if you can. I don't want Mugsy to see it. I'll throw it into the back of my truck."

"I'll do that for you."

"It's two blocks away in the parking lot next to the German Meat Market. You don't have to do it."

"It's not a bother. I'll have a stretch for my legs and while I'm gone you can see if you can coax Mugsy out of the cage."

"Thanks. Tell the kid who's taking the money that it's the Ford pick-up truck – a red F-150 Raptor SVT" Muldoon shouted back.

"Yep. I know that kid. He's my son Patrick....works there on Saturdays."

By the time Kitty returned, Muldoon had made enough friendly tones to Mugsy that he came out of the cage --- very, very cautiously --- but out of it just the same. He was still, after five weeks, a little wobbly on his legs and somewhat gun-shy of Muldoon's tender ovations to stand next to him. But the dog did walk out with his new owner to the front of the pound leaving all that obvious misery behind him.

Kitty gave Muldoon the name of the local vet who would give Mugsy his necessary shots. "Don't you think he's likely had them all already?"

"Muldoon, whatever shots this poor dog had in his previous life has probably long since disappeared from his system considering his condition and all. Besides, you'll need to get to know Doc Carlin well anyway. He's the only vet in town."

"Any good is he?"

"I've watched him bring many a nearly dead animal straight back to life over the years – he's the best. We're lucky to have him living in this town."

"OK...I'll make contact with him"

Kitty stood watch over Mugsy as Muldoon went to get his pick-up from the parking lot after deciding that even the two shorts blocks to walk would be too much of a strain on the dog's present state of health.

After they both managed to gently place Mugsy in the front seat, Kitty reminded Muldoon that there was a very nice pet store on the way out of town where he could get all the necessaries for setting his new dog up comfortably in the cabin.

Before he drove off, Muldoon reached over from the driver's seat and gave Kitty a substantial donation to the dog pound.

"$300 dollars!!...that's way too much Muldoon!" Kitty

exclaimed.

"Mugsy's worth every penny! Thanks for all your help, Kitty. I'll see you around."

As Kitty watched him drive off she said "God was good to that dog today. That Muldoon Frickey is a real nice guy. Mugsy's gone and found himself a real good home."

Chapter Five

After spending the rest of Saturday and all day Sunday close by Mugsy's side, by Monday morning Muldoon could see that he was beginning to show some signs of improvement.

Doc Carlin was a great help. When Muldoon phoned him as soon as he got the dog home on Saturday afternoon, the Doc volunteered to drive out to the lake and have a look at him. He gave Muldoon a special blend of dog food and medicine that he said would put him on the road to recovery. Mugsy ate some without too much fuss and drank a lot of water.

By 10:30 on Monday morning, after their early morning breakfast together, Muldoon decided that it would be OK to leave Mugsy alone in the house for a few hours while he went to the office and started work on those background checks that Gerry Dowling faxed to him.

"Gotta go, Mugsy 'ol boy. Gotta go earn my daily bread if I am going to be able to keep us living in the lap of luxury here!" he laughed. "You can be in charge of the cabin while I am gone. OK?" Muldoon went up stairs, leaping them two at a time, to get his wallet and coat. When he came back into the kitchen to grab his keys, Mugsy was standing up with this look on his face that said "Where you go, I go."

So, off they both went to the offices of Muldoon Frickey:

Private Investigator.

Muldoon worked away as diligently and as competently as ever while Mugsy took a long snooze on the floor next to the fax machine. A lot of the background checks were for employment purposes and didn't require going "deep". He found a few snags in a couple of them and faxed them right away to Gerry. A few of the others were for on-going fraud investigations and took a little longer and Muldoon knew exactly what red flags to look for. He spent the last seven of his twenty years on the force in the Fraud Unit. He always thought it was amazing what people thought they could get away with. "Sooner or later it always catches up with them." he muttered.

He noticed one name on a request sheet from Gerry that he recognized immediately. Yevgrev Andreovitch, a Russian con-man with "more money than sense" as Muldoon always referred to him. "I thought we busted him good just before I left the force. I seem to remember that he was in the slammer working out a plea agreement with the District Attorney." Muldoon recollected that on the night of his good-bye party from the force, the staff from the Fraud Unit was buying him shot after shot of Patron tequila for having brought Andreovitch to his knees. "How could he be out just two and a half years years later and running another scheme?" wondered Muldoon. Running the kind of check that Gerry wanted on the Russian took Muldoon two hours. When he was finished he sent it straight away to Gerry with a note saying "How'd this guy get out so soon? Thanks for the biz. Talk to you soon."

By the time he finished with all of Gerry's work it was four o'clock and time for Mugsy's medicine. "Let's go, boy – time to go home and get you feelin' good again. You can have your medicine and a little grub and I am truly parched for a cold one."

Muldoon took care to get Mugsy safely in the truck for the

half a mile drive home. "Maybe we'll watch an old movie tonight…
how 'bout that Mugsy….sound like a plan to you? I bet you like
Clint Eastwood, don't you? Yeah…..I'll just bet you do. We'll
have a look at "Play Misty for Me"…how 'bout that?"

Because Mugsy didn't disagree, Muldoon automatically put
him in the "I like Clint" club.

Before long, Mugsy and Muldoon were having their own version of "Monday Night at the Movies" with no clue that Gerry
sent a one-page fax back to Muldoon's office at 6:00 pm that read
"Good work, as ususal. Call me ASAP. Very important."

———————

The next morning Muldoon had to insist to Mugsy that he
stay home while he took a drive into town to do some shopping
and check a few things out. Mugsy looked determined to follow
him out the door until Muldoon laid all his blankets out next to
the fireplace hearth and said "Be a good dog and stay. I'm bringing
back a whole bunch of treats from the pet store for you." Mugsy
didn't seem too happy about it, but he stayed put anyway. "I'll be
back in time for your afternoon medicine."

Muldoon drove right past his office. If he had made a quick
stop in there he would have seen the second fax from Gerry that
arrived at 7:00 am which said: "Need to talk soon."

He got to the pet store in no time at all and pulled into the
parking lot in the back. When he walked inside, he was surprised
at the size and variety of the inventory. He stood there wondering
which way to turn.

"You look like you need some help." said the pretty blond sales
assistant.

"Excuse me?"

"You look confused. Can I help you with anything." she
repeated while she gave the handsome P.I. the once over.

Muldoon smiled his killer smile at her and said "I need a leash."

"Oh.....I'll just bet you *do!*" she replied with her hands resting easily on her curvy hips.

"For my dog" added Muldoon.

"Well, you *are* in a pet store, sir."

"Can you point me in the right direction?"

"All the way in the back on the left. They're hanging on the wall. Let me know if you don't see what you need."

Muldoon found himself staring at a wall full of too many leashes until another sales assistant approached him. "Can I help you with anything?" Muldoon looked at his name tag pinned to his uniform shirt. "Well, Robert....I'll tell you....I just got a dog and I am looking for a leash."

Robert pointed to the wall and said matter-of-factly "This is it."

"By any chance to you sell leather leashes here, Robert?"

"No....I don't think anybody even makes them anymore, sir. Everyone likes these retractable ones now days. It lets the dog run ahead of you for a bit, but you can but an end to the romp by pressing the button on the handle."

"But you don't sell the leather ones."

"Nope" answered Robert "not since I've been here and that's going on six years now." Muldoon rubbed his chin for a second. "Why do you want a leather leash anyway? They're far too restrictive on the animal. The dog's never more than four or five feet from you. I think people who use them must be control freaks or something – no disrespect intended, sir."

"None taken, Robert. No worries. I'll take one of the retractables then. So, no other pet store will carry them either, will they?"

"This is the only pet store for miles – but I really doubt if anyone else will have one."

"You have a dog, Robert?"

"Sure do – I have two Golden Labs – just beautiful, too. They love the retractable leash. What breed of dog do you have – if you don't mind my asking?"

"An Irish Wolfhound" said Muldoon "just got him".

Robert looked at him very strangely. "You can't put an Irish Wolfhound on a leather leash! It's inhuman."

"I was really given a bad piece of advice, wasn't I, Robert?"

"I should say so, sir. I'm glad you stopped by my department."

"Well, thanks for setting me straight. I can pay up front?"

"Right up front. sir. Have a nice day. By the way, the park at the end of Main Street has a nice big dog run, if you are interested."

Muldoon nodded and headed towards the front of the store. "Haven't sold them in six years? Where the hell did that leather leash come from then?" he wondered.

Chapter Six

The street and foot traffic on Main Street was a sight different than what Muldoon witnessed on Saturday. There was almost no traffic, save a few 18-wheelers headed down to the depot and the sidewalks were virtually empty except for a few senior citizens and some young mothers pushing strollers. One lady walking merrily along was pushing a light-weight doll stroller with a stuffed toy rabbit in it….nothing else….just the toy rabbit. Muldoon shook his head and thought not only that "it takes all kinds" but also where we'd be "if everybody was the same." He thought he'd probably be out of work. No need for investigations if each person was just like the next.

It was easy for him to park at a meter close to The Belly Up. He made sure his truck was locked because the retractable leash was inside along with every conceivable type of dog pillow, cushy mattress bed, blanket, flavored gnawing bone and several boxes of treat dog biscuits. That piece of information that Robert, the sales attendant, gave him about leather leashes wound up costing him over $400 in dog "furnishings". Muldoon didn't mind. "My Mugsy's from a regal breed and I am going to let him live like a king." he said.

He felt pretty regal himself when he walked into The Belly Up and heard Patti-cake shout from the middle of the bar "Hey there handsome – were you been?"

"Hiya Patti-cake" he replied thinking that God probably only made two or three women in history with a figure like that.

"Haven't seen you in a few days – having your usual?"

Muldoon wasn't going to fall for that twice. "No thanks, hon – how about just a cold Sam Adams. I'll save the martini for another time."

"Comin' your way" she said as she reached in the cooler for a Sam and brought it right up to Muldoon. "I was thinking you might not come back. Like maybe we scared you off or something."

"I don't scare Patti-cake – ever. Besides, with a good-looking woman like you behind that bar, I'm surprised I didn't move in on that first day!"

"Who's moving in with you Patti-cake?" bellowed the tall bearded gent who just strolled into The Belly Up. "Better not be anybody but me!!" he jested

"Hey, Ken. I guess you're not flying anywhere today."

"You got that right, darlin'. Other wise why would I be in here before the middle of the afternoon looking for a cold Budweiser?"

Ken took a perch on one of the bar stools and laid his daily newspaper next to him. He was a helicopter pilot and he took anybody and everybody, smooth as silk, up in his chopper. Norwegian by ancestry and a top notch pilot by design, Ken was the best in Belleva County.

"Muldoon" said Patti-cake "you gotta meet Ken here. He knows everybody in this town, don't you Ken?"

"I guess I do – been around long enough." said Ken.

Muldoon reached out to shake his hand and said that he had just moved up here from the big city. "Is that right?" said Ken "I'm down there sometimes two or three times a week. You should fly down with me sometime."

"What kind of chopper do you have?"

"Ah....it's a beaut. It's so beautiful, I'd sleep in it if I could. I bought a Bell 407 a few months ago. It's like having a sports car in the air, believe me. Seats seven and cruises at 140 kn."

"Who's flying someplace?" asked the next man to waltz through the door. It was Doc Carlin. He recognized Muldoon right away and took a stool in between him and Ken.

"Hi Doc!" shouted Patti-cake from the other end of the bar. "You having your usual?"

"I don't see why not. I know you'll give it to me whether I want it or not!"

"Just let me finish up down here."

By "finishing up down here", she meant she had to pour Larry Lutursky another shot of whiskey and give him another bottle of beer while trying to coax any kind of conversation from him in the process. Getting him the beer and whiskey was easy. Getting him to say anything was not, but Patti-cake had long since gotten used to Larry's sullen behavior. She gave him what he ordered and left him alone. It would be more fun at the other end of the bar. Some of her favorite customers were now here and she could stand close to Muldoon without feeling self-conscious. "By God, he's a handsome man." she thought to herself.

By the time she walked from one end of the bar to the other, Barry the Gambler rushed in and shouted "Christ, did any of you guys hear what happened??

"Is this another one of your big announcements, Barry – like the traffic light just changed from red to green?" scowled Ken.

Barry ignored him. "I'm not kidding. This is serious!" he continued to shout. "it looks like a couple of kids mighta got murdered last night."

Muldoon took a long swig of his beer and listened closely but didn't say a word.

"What are you rambling about?" said Ken

"Two teenagers living over by the park. They must have been in the boy's house because I heard it was his mother who found them naked in bed – dead as doornails, the both of them."

"Dead from what?" asked Doc.

"Drugs! It was drugs...a drug death." claimed Barry.

"And they murdered each other with drugs....is that what you're telling us?" said Ken incredulously.

"I'm only telling you what I heard!" said Barry.

"That's the trouble with you and your announcements, Barry. You come in here with half-assed information and nobody can make sense of it. And you wonder why nobody pays you any mind!" scolded Ken

"Who were these kids, anyway?" asked Patti-cake "and how old were they?"

"I don't really know that..." admitted Barry

Ken looked at both Muldoon and Doc "See what I mean?"

"All I know is that I just seen Chief Branderford coming out of the diner on the corner and I heard him say that the kid was a known "druggie".

"Muldoon" said Patti-cake "you're an investigator....what does this sound like to you?"

"I'll tell you what it doesn't sound like...."

Muldoon was interrupted by the sound of the shot glass Larry was holding crashing to the floor. Everybody looked in his direction and he got up from his seat, grabbed his cane and walked out the back door.

"That guy has a tendency to leave the bar at the oddest moments" thought Muldoon.

Both Doc and Ken waived him off as though they were used to strange behavior from Larry.

"Anyway...you were saying Muldoon..." Doc chirped in.

"Oh…I was just saying that it doesn't sound like Barry has a full set of facts."

"He never does!!! That's my point. He's exasperating." said an obviously exasperated Ken.

"But, two teenagers dead from any kind of drug use right under the mother's nose leads me to believe that something strange was going on." added Muldoon.

"Hey, Muldoon" said Ken "you're new here…but if you stick around this town long enough and you'll learn that a *lot* of strange things happen here!"

Chapter Seven

Muldoon thought about what Ken said on his way home. Teenagers overdosing on drugs was nothing new to him. He'd seen too much of it in the big city. This was different, though. This was a small town. He wondered how the hell any supply of drugs found their way up here. He had to think that the two kids who died were not alone in their drug use. "Must be others" he said "shame about those kids though. Parents never get over that kind of thing. Nobody raises their kids thinking they're going to wind up dead from drugs."

He pulled in front of his office and threw his truck into "park" and hopped out. He saw his landlord, George Butterman, walk around from the far side of the building and he waived. He did not feel the need to engage him in conversation. "He gets my rent from me. That's about all he needs."

When he walked into his office, the first thing he saw was the new pile of faxes in the fax tray. He smiled. "Good 'ol Gerry" he said as he began to sift through them. He felt a sudden uncomfortable feeling when he saw the two faxes asking that Muldoon contact his old pal "ASAP". He put the faxes down immediately and picked up his office phone and punched in Gerry's number on the touch-tone pad.

"Hello" said the woman answering Muldoon's call "Mr.

Dowling's office."

"Is he there, please? This is Mr. Frickey calling...Muldoon Frickey".

"Oh, yes....Mr. Frickey.....Mr. Dowling had been expecting your call yesterday. I'm afraid he's out of the office just now and can't be reached. He'll return in a few hours. Would you like me to tell him that you phoned?"

"Please do" replied Muldoon "tell him I am sorry for the delay but I only just saw his urgent fax just now. I was pre-occupied with personal business yesterday and couldn't stop in my office to check for faxes. I didn't want Gerry to think I was ignoring him."

But Muldoon didn't want Gerry to know that he spent his day shopping for dog blankets and trying to put the moves on a pretty Greek barmaid, either.

"Alright, Mr. Frickey....I'll let Mr. Dowling know."

"And what is your name, please?" asked Muldoon.

"Louise....Louise Rainer. I'm Mr. Dowling's new secretary."

"Oh, that's nice" replied Muldoon "you're working for a great guy."

"Thank you, Mr. Frickey. He's a nice boss and I'm settling in just fine."

"How long have you been working for him, if I may ask.... and by the way, you can call me Muldoon. Gerry and I are old friends."

"Going on two months now....and *you* can call me Louise."

"OK, Louise. Nice talking to you. I'll try calling again later."

"Very good, Muldoon. Good-bye".

After he hung up, Muldoon wondered if he should hire a secretary. "Naw" was his own reply "I don't need any distractions." He knew himself too well.

After Muldoon gave Mugsy his afternoon medicine mixed in with a few treats, he sat down at the kitchen table and began to gently brush Mugsy's coat with one of the four different brushes he bought at the pet store. As long as he brushed softly, Mugsy stayed pretty still. He only began to flinch when Muldoon ran the brush too firmly over the area where Kitty speculated that he might have been beaten – over on the left side where his now-healed cracked ribs were. "Easy boy…easy now. I won't hurt you." he said reassuringly.

He picked up a different, smaller brush to work on Mugsy's throat. "You know Mugsy, 'ol pal, I know it's only been a few days but I think Doc Carlin's medicine is already starting to show some positive effect on you. You're eyes are a whole lot clearer than when I first brought you home and you're sitting up pretty good. Must be that Irish breeding of yours…..you can survive anything. Yeah, you're a tough old hound, aren't you?"

When Muldoon turned to the side to drop the small brush on the table and get a different one for the legs and paws, Mugsy moved his head right in and licked Muldoon's face. Not once, but three times.

Muldoon responded by placing Mugsy's head in his two hands and rubbed the top of his head very cautiously. "Yeah… that right Mugsy…you good old hound. It's you and me. We're going to be real good pals….I just know it. You and me. We'll take good care of each other."

Muldoon heard his cell phone ringing which he set next to the sink on the other side of the kitchen. He thought it might, by chance, be Gerry calling back already. He stepped around Mugsy to grab the phone before it went to voice-mail.

"Hello" he said.

"Is this Mr. Frickey?" asked the woman's voice.

"It sure is.....this is Muldoon Frickey. Who's this?"

"Mr. Frickey my name is Wanda Skudnick. I got your number from Doc Carlin." she said with a little quiver in her voice.

"Ok...ok...." he replied wondering what the connection was "I know Doc Carlin...he's been helping me take care of my dog."

"Yes, sir...that's what he told me. He works a lot with Kitty Selarus....you know...Kitty from the dog pound? Kitty's my best girlfriend from high school."

"Ok...ok...I'm with you. What can I do for you Mrs. Skudnick?....is it 'Mrs.'?"

There was a pause and Muldoon thought he could hear something akin to crying from the other end of the phone connection. "Is it 'Mrs.' or 'Miss'?" he asked again. More pauses. "Are you there?" he asked trying to remain professional.

"Yes...yes, sir. I'm still here." she replied haltingly "It's Mrs. Skudnick...I'm divorced but it's still Mrs. Skudnick."

Muldoon sensed that this Mrs. Skudnick was trying mightily to compose herself.

"How can I help you?"

"Well, you see Mr. Frickey...it's my son....I mean...it's about my son, Paul. It's very hard to talk about.....you see..."

"Just take your time, Mrs. Skudnick. I'm not going anywhere. Is your son missing?"

Now Muldoon could hear what he definitely recognized as crying. "Try to stay calm ." he said "Is this about your missing son?"

"He's not missing, Mr. Frickey.....he's dead. I think somebody killed my boy."

She began to cry uncontrollably. In his repeated attempts to calm her down, Muldoon wondered if this was the same boy whose death was loudly announced to everyone in The Belly Up by Barry the Gambler.

Finally, Mrs. Skudnick was able to speak again. "Doc told me you were an investigator, Mr. Frickey." She began to sob again. "I.....I...h...have m..m...money. I can.....I can pay you."

"Let's not talk about money right away, Mrs. Skudnick. I would be willing to meet with you so I can get the facts straight."

"I just want to know who killed my boy with those drugs." she croaked.

It sure sounded like the kid in the announcement that Barry got half right and half wrong.

"Tell me where you live and I can come to your house so we can talk about this. I won't be able to do it until tomorrow afternoon at the earliest, though."

"I'm burying my boy tomorrow, Mr. Frickey.....my only child....seventeen years old and I have to bury him. You can't know what that's like."

"I'm very sorry for your loss, Mrs. Skudnick. If it's convenient, why don't we meet on Friday?"

"No. Come Thursday. I want to find out who did this to my boy.....the sooner the better."

And so it was agreed. Muldoon Frickey: Private Investigator would meet with Mrs. Wanda Skutnick: Grieving Mother. ....to talk about her dead son.

Muldoon placed the cell phone back on the counter near the sink and walked back over to the kitchen table where Mugsy was patiently waiting. "So...Mugsy" he said "looks like we might have our first big case! I think you are bringing me Irish luck, you old hound dog you!"

Chapter Eight

Before Thursday afternoon's meeting with Mrs. Skudnick rolled around, Muldoon made sure to make contact with Gerry Dowling. It was brief because he was on the run, as usual, and he asked Muldoon if he could make it down to the big city on Sunday to have a chat about something that Gerry said "I don't want to talk about over the phone." Muldoon agreed but told Gerry that he didn't want to have to drive down and back on the same day.

"So stay overnight – what's the problem? I'll have the company put you up in a nice hotel. Louise, my secretary will arrange it all."

Muldoon explained about Mugsy and said he didn't want to leave him alone overnight just yet. "He's coming along just great but I'd rather not leave him alone. But, I met a guy in town here – a helicopter pilot – who is very used to flying his chopper back and forth."

"OK, pal…if that works for you, it's fine with me. We'll pay for it." Settled.

Now all he had to do was see if Ken was free to make the flight on Sunday.

"I'll make a quick stop at The Belly Up to see how I can contact him and then I want to go over to the dog pound, too. I want to talk to Kitty about her friend Wanda."

He wanted to look professional for his meeting so after he put on his white shirt, jacket and tie, Muldoon was ready to go. And from the looks of it, so was Mugsy. He was sitting at the front door when Muldoon came down the stairs.

"Uh...uh...no...no....no, my friend....not this time. Mugsy stood up and waited for Muldoon to open the door. Muldoon noticed that his tail was wagging a little bit. "Well...first time I've seen that! But, no.....you are going to stay here and guard the cabin for me for a few hours."

He coaxed him over to the cushy padded dog mattress near the fireplace and gave him a few treats to gnaw on for a while. "You stay put while I go and do my private investigator thing."

There was not a soul in The Belly Up when Muldoon walked in – not even any sign of anyone behind the bar. Muldoon was glad for the absence of patrons but was disappointed not to see Patti-cake tending bar. Even without any customers calling for drinks, the bar retained an unexplainable, unique character all its own that makes for a good local watering hole. It was just the right size...not too big or too small. Not too dark....old fashioned ceiling fans and room enough between the bar stools and the wall so that nobody was falling into each other when the bar got crowded at Happy Hour, which it inevitably did whether Patti-cake was behind the bar – but especially if she was.

There were signs along the wall offering all sorts of different kinds of cocktails – a special one for every day, Monday through Friday, at knocked-down prices. But, as eye-catching as those signs were, The Belly-Up was a basically shot 'n a beer bar. Nothing too fancy. The jukebox must have had 10,000 songs in it, but it was usually Country & Western during the day and whatever loud, unmelodic screeching junk the younger crowd liked to play at night. It was definitely a bar that held a little something for everybody.

Muldoon's disappointment was short-lived when he saw Patti-cake come up from downstairs carrying a case of Budweiser. "Can I help you with that?" he said.

His presence took Patti-cake by surprise. "Well hello there Handsome Man! I thought I was all alone in here." "Thank God I'm not anymore" was her silent thought. She wondered, just for a second, if Muldoon just looked so damn handsome in comparison to some of her other customers or was it that he *really was* just so stand-on-his-own strikingly attractive.

"Well, I won't say 'no' to a nice offer like that." she replied "if you could just carry this case up to where you are standing, I'll load it in the cooler...don't muss up your nice shirt, tho." Muldoon grabbed the case of beer like it weighed two pounds and gave her a look that said 'No worries'.

"Quiet morning?" he asked

"Ah....it's just getting started. You want something to drink or are you passing through....you look awfully nice all slicked up in that jacket and tie.....sure doesn't look like a 'drinkin' outfit' to me" she said with a laugh.

Muldoon explained that he had a meeting in an hour with Wanda Skudnick and Patti-cake replied "Yeah...I know Wanda.... she used to come in here on a regular basis looking for her husband, who usually high-tailed it out of here whenever somebody told him that his wife was on her way."

"He was a regular here, then?"

"My 'regulars' are mostly good-natured drinkers – admittedly, some drink a lot more than others – but my daytime crowed is good natured most of the time. Wally Skudnick was just a nasty-ass alcoholic...had a really bad foul mouth on him, too. Called his wife all sorts of names including the one you should *NEVER* call a woman.....whether she is one or not.

"Why did you let him continue to come in here?" asked

Muldoon

"Pietro banned him twice and he would always worm his way back into his good graces, I guess. But it was never very long before he went back to his old ways again. I could never prove it but I swear he would go into the guy's bathroom and snort a few lines of coke. Pietro said unless I could get proof, there was nothing he could do. There are no cameras in the bathrooms so I was stuck serving him."

"You never just cut him off?"

"I did one time and he raised holy hell – called me every name in the book – threatened to kill me if I didn't give him another drink."

"What happened?"

"Ken…you remember meeting Ken – he's the helicopter pilot?" Muldoon nodded.

"Well Ken gets up from his bar stool walks over…grabs Wally by the neck and threw him bodily out the back door. Told him never to step foot in the bar again whenever he was there. Told him he never wanted to see his face or hear his voice again."

"Ken's a pretty big guy, too!" laughed Muldoon

"Yeah, that's for sure! And Wally Skudnick was a puny little guy…..surprisingly big mouth for such a little man." added Patti-cake.

"Ever see him again after that?"

"Not once…..and that was about a month ago. He drank worse after Wanda divorced him which, I think, was about two years ago."

"You have quite a few characters in this place, don't you?'

"Muldoon, you have *no* idea!" she said again with that beguiling Melena Mercouri laugh of hers. There was a crippling charm to it and Muldoon was falling prey.

"Maybe you'll tell me all about them one time."

"You never stay long enough!" Patti-cake protested.

"Well.....I do have a job outside this bar and I have to get going right now....but before I go can you tell me how I can contact Ken? I want to ask him about some flight arrangements."

"Easy enough......if he doesn't come in by two or three o'clock, he won't be in at all. It means he's flying somewhere. If it's the case that he doesn't come in, I'll send him a text and tell him to call you. What's your telephone number? Where you going anyway?'

"What are you – a private detective or something?" he jested.

Patti-cake said nothing but stood up straight and tossed her brown hair back with one hand and jetted her chest out a little."

"Maybe I'll tell *you* all about it one day!!" he said trying not to be so obvious about looking so obviously straight at her.

"Like I said, handsome......you never stay long enough." Muldoon smelled an opening.

"Well....maybe dinner then...sometime?"

Patti-cake shifted her hips ever so naturally and continued to load the Budweiser into the cooler.

"Maybe" was all she said.

Chapter Nine

It must have been nap time at the dog pound because when Muldoon walked in he didn't find it necessary to raise his voice in conversation above the din of the sometimes repetitive, often staccato and always loud barking of dogs looking for a home or trying to get a stay of execution. Kitty was seated at the front desk entering data from paperwork onto the on-line version of the "available" dogs for rescue.

"Afternoon , Kitty. How are you?"

She greeted him more enthusiastically than she would any other customer dropping in. "Oh my heavens!! Muldoon! What a nice surprise. How nice to see you. What brings you back to our pound?......looking for a mate for Mugsy?" she said with a bright smile.

"Well.....not just yet.....I think I'll wait 'till he's fully back on his feet again --- although you'd be surprised Kitty – he's looking ten times better than when I picked him up here last week....I think Doc Carlin must be some kind of miracle worker or something."

"Didn't I tell you!!...Didn't I just tell you that he was capable of bringing dogs back from the brink of disaster.....didn't I?"

Muldoon gave Kitty credit where credit was due and thanked her again for all her help. "Doc's in the back right now looking over a few of our dogs....let me go get him."

Muldoon stopped her and said that he wanted to have a private chat with her before he gave an impromptu report to Doc on Mugsy's progress.

"I wanted to have a word with you, if I could about, your friend Wanda Skudnick. She phoned me the other night and I am going to meet her in a half an hour up at her house."

Kitty just shook her head in sadness. "Poor Wanda.....she can't get a break. It seems like she's stuck in a tough life."

"She told me that you and she have been friends since high school." said Muldoon

"Best friends....since the first day of high school. Wanda's always had a tough time of things."

"How do you mean?" asked Muldoon

"She had a bad home life and seemed to repeat the disaster in her married life. Her father was a terrible drunk and used to smack Wanda and her mother around all the time. Then she went and married that snake, Wally, who was worse. And the pity of it is that Wanda's a real sweet woman...real nice to people and a wonderful friend. But her whole life has been a tar pit of bad men."

"What about the boy....her son, Paul?"

"He was the absolute love of her life...her angel. And a nice kid, too. He and my son, Patrick, were good friends.....both on the wrestling team.....hung out together....until...well, until.... you know.

Muldoon nodded but did not say anything.

"That funeral on Tuesday was the saddest spectacle you could imagine. A desert could have been flooded with the amount of tears shed at that church. It was just awful. I don't know how Wanda made it through."

"Was her ex-husband there?"

Kitty's voice turned cold. "He wouldn't have dared! Even

when they were still married, Wanda had to raise that boy all by herself….Wally never helped with anything. And after the divorce, he always fell behind in his support payments."

"No alimony?"

"From *that* loser??…..Wanda knew she'd go blue waiting for an alimony check so she never even asked for any. No…she was already keeping body and soul together from her own job. She didn't want anything from him for herself but she expected that he might keep up on his child support…..but I guess that was too much to ask from a deadbeat drunk like him."

Muldoon scratched his head a bit trying to soak all this in and appeared perplexed.

"Seemingly nice kid…well liked…loved by his mother….high school athlete…..what's he doing mixed up in drugs?….and what's he doing bringing a sixteen-year old girl into a shady deal like that?….something doesn't make sense to me."

Kitty stood up, not crying, but visibly upset. "That's what a lot of people think, Muldoon. It just *doesn't* make sense! And now this sweet young boy is dead and my friend, Wanda, feels like killing herself. It's just a horrible disaster."

Muldoon thought for a minute and said "Kitty, would you mind if I talked to your son, Patrick, about Paul Skudnick?

"No…not at all. I can have him here 'round closing time if you want."

Muldoon didn't know how long the meeting with Wanda would take and he also wanted to get back to his office and finish up the new work for Gerry…plus he had to get home to give Mugsy his afternoon medicine. "Not today, Kitty…I have too much to do. Will he be at the parking lot on Saturday?"

"All day" replied Kitty "until five o'clock in the evening."

"OK….I'll have a chat with him then. I'm coming into town on Saturday anyway. I want to get some of those smoked pork chops at the German Meat Market. I've heard they are pretty good."

"Best on earth!!" It was Doc Carlin just walking in from the back room. "None better.….you don't even have to cook 'em.….you can bite right in!"

Muldoon reached out to shake Doc's hand. "How are you, Doc?"

"Fit as a fiddle for a man of my advancing years!"

"G'wan Doc.…you're not a day over 50 are you?" said Muldoon with a wink.

"Ah.…would that it were so, my good man.….would that it were so, but you are twenty years shy of the mark. How's the patient, by the way?"

"I was just telling Kitty here, that he looks ten times better than he did when I first brought him home. It's very gratifying to watch him get stronger every day."

"I should probably come out your way and give him a good looking over. Might be time to adjust the medication if he's doing as well as you say he is. How about sometime on Sunday?"

"I can't this Sunday, Doc. I'm going down to the big city.… which reminds me.…if you see Ken in The Belly Up later can you tell him that I would like him to chopper me down there on Sunday, if he's available?"

"I know he's not flying today" said Doc "because I saw him in the grocery store earlier this morning. So if I see him at the bar, I'll give him your number – if that's all right with you."

"That'd be great. Thanks, Doc." Muldoon turned to Kitty "Thanks for the chat, Kitty. I'll see you again."

"Always good to see you, Muldoon. Take care." she replied "do what you can for Wanda, OK?"

"I'll do my best."

Chapter Ten

The meeting with Wanda Skudnick lasted almost two hours. The understandably upset and bereaved mother kept rambling on and on. Muldoon tried to keep her on track but she kept going off on tangents, some of which had very little to do with her dead son. But, if twenty years on the force taught him anything, Muldoon knew enough to try and listen to everything. He learned as a rookie that you'd never know when odd pieces of information are going to connect and start making sense.

Wanda had a copy of the coroner's report that she got from a friend in the Coroner's Office. Muldoon was surprised that she had it.

"There's something wrong with that simpleton going around telling anybody that Paul was a known "druggie"."

"Are you talking about Chief Branderford -- Peter Branderford?"

"Yes. He's an idiot. My son was not into drugs. I know that for as sure as I am standing here. The person they are talking about in the coroner's report and my boy are not the same."

"But, Mrs. Skudnick…the report says he died from a lethal dose of ecstasy…ecstasy is a dangerous drug…one pill can be fatal."

"I want you to find out who gave it to him…..find out where

my boy got that pill."

"All due respect, Mrs. Skudnick....maybe he just went out and bought it. Teenagers in the big city buy it like bubble gum. It's everywhere."

"This is NOT the big city" she screamed "and my Paul was not like those teenagers. He was a good boy. Somebody gave him that pill -- I want to know who!!!" She broke down in sobs for the third time.

Muldoon tried to calm her down again. "Why would Chief Branderford spread a rumor about your son if it was not true?"

"I think he hates the teenagers. He terrorizes the kids in this town. He's been doing it for over two years. Most of them are scared to death of him. They can't even hang out on the corner to make after school plans without him driving up with the red light flashing threatening to arrest them if they don't break it up."

Muldoon didn't mention that he and the Chief used to be partners. It wasn't information that Wanda needed to know. "What about the girl? Do you know anything about her? Do you have the coroner's report on her?"

Wanda shook her head. "I don't know much about her. Her name was Esperanza...I can't remember her last name. She was not from Paul's high school."

The way Muldoon left it with Wanda was that he'd make some preliminary inquiries and if he came up with anything interesting, she'd have to start paying an hourly rate for him to continue. She agreed and they left it at that.

By the time he raced home, it was already 4:30 pm -- past time for Mugsy's afternoon dose of medicine. "Hey there, 'ol boy – did you think I forgot about you? Nothin' doin'...not a chance!"

Mugsy was in full tail wag and glad to see the Master of the

House. He scarfed down the small bowl of food and meal that Doc recommended with the medicine mixed in. Muldoon gave him a couple of biscuit treats after that and they both settled in the living room where Muldoon wanted to put his feet up and think about his next move to try and unravel the death of young Paul Skudnick.

He started to doze off in the middle of planning his strategy when his cell phone rang. He did not recognize the number being displayed so he used his deep, officious tone.

"Mr. Frickey here. How can I help you?"

"Muldoon?......it's Ken.....from The Belly Up....the helicopter pilot."

"Hey, Ken....how are you? Sorry....I didn't mean to sound so officious....I didn't recognize your number."

"I saw Doc in the bar this afternoon and he said I ought to give you a call."

"Right.....right.....I was looking for you earlier. I was wondering if you could chopper me down to the big city on Sunday? I have to be there by 1:00 pm and then I'll need you to bring me back the same day....probably around 5:00 – no later than 6:00 for certain."

"No problem" said Ken without hesitation " I'll book you out for the whole day."

Ken told Muldoon where to meet him and they sealed the deal.

"He knows just about everyone in this town, too" reflected Muldoon "I'll just bet he has some thoughts about Paul and Wanda Skudnick."

Back at The Belly Up the Happy Hour crowd was getting loud and Patti-cake was having a good time. There was nothing she liked better than a full bar. People would be having a good time and she'd be making some nice tips.

"Darlin' can you get me another bottle of Bud when you come down this way?" shouted Ken "and get Doc what he wants, too."

"Anything for you guys" she replied. Ken got up from his seat and headed for the men's bathroom but stopped at the juke on the way to thrown in a dollar and rev the crowd up with "I Walk the Line" and "Ring of Fire" by Johnny Cash – always big crowd pleasers at The Belly Up.

He walked around the corner to the rest rooms and saw Larry Lutursky coming out of the Ladies' Room.

"Use the Men's you old perv." growled Ken. He was just as tall as Larry and 18 years younger and had a mean stare when he felt like it.

"Somebody was in there and I had to go." snapped Larry "and it ain't your business."

"Well….I'm *makin'* it my business…..stay out of the Ladies' Room."

Larry returned Ken's evil stare, walked back to the bar, threw down his shot of Jack and walked out the back door….hat on his head and cane in his hand.

When Ken got back to his seat he still had a scowl on his face. "What's eating you?" asked Doc

"I really don't like that Lutursky guy…..I mean *really* don't like him."

"Ken" answered Doc "you haven't liked him in about forty years….what's the beef?"

"I just saw him walk out of the Ladies'Room….what's with that?"

Patti-cake overheard the exchange and gave an exaggerated shudder. "I've seen him do that before" she said "gives me the creeps to think of him in there."

"You're making too much of it." said Doc "maybe he's got a weak bladder."

"I think he's got a weak brain" concluded Ken.

"One day Peitro will finally toss him out of here for good." said Doc

"None too soon for me. He never causes fights but his whole presence in this bar just doesn't fit …….. especially at night with the younger crowd." said Patti-cake.

"This is it….just what I mean." said Ken swallowing the last of his beer "why is a guy like that in here at night?"

"Who knows?" said Doc "maybe he's got nowhere else to go."

"What's wrong with the cemetery? --- permanent like."

Chapter Eleven

Normally Muldoon did not make a habit of working at night.

It was his adverse reaction to too many nights of stakeouts while on the force. There were times when he thought he'd never be able to enjoy the light of day again. The force was turning him into a night owl. It was case after case that required stakeout after stakeout. Those were the days when he was partnered with Peter Branderford. Muldoon hadn't thought of it in awhile – there was no need to – but he had a recollection that Peter was a little rough with some of the suspects and knocked around more than a few of their confidential informants. Street "CIs" were usually of questionable character to begin with, but Peter would get really pissed off with some of them when their information didn't pan out. He belted them around. Muldoon always had to remind him that without the CIs, they'd be getting no information at all. Peter always accused Muldoon of playing it "too much by the book". "That's our job" was Muldoon's standard response.

When he got the news that his request to join the elite Fraud Unit was granted, Muldoon was just as happy to bid his three year partnership with Peter goodbye. They got along well enough but Muldoon realized that they had a different approach to law enforcement. Besides, Muldoon was looking for an escape route from the endless string of girlfriends that Peter's wife, Jennifer, was always trying to fix him up with. Jennie was determined to get Muldoon married and he was determined to remain single. Not only did Muldoon not want to end his bachelor days, he especially did not want the kind of marriage Peter and Jennifer had. It seemed to him that they were always fighting.....at least that's the way it seemed when he had to listen endlessly to Peter's complaining all through the night – on stakeout after stakeout.

Peter got a new partner and Muldoon headed off to spend his last seven years on the force in the Fraud Unit.

But tonight it was off to the office to wrap up the rest of his assignments for Gerry Dowling. He wanted everything completed before he went down to the big city on Sunday to have his meeting. So after dinner he brought Mugsy with him to the office. Muldoon would have preferred to leave him at home but after having left him on his own all afternoon, he was feeling a bit guilty. And, Mugsy seemed in no mood to continue to "be in charge of the cabin" and practically plopped himself on top of Muldoon as he tried to finish his dinner while watching the sports highlights on tv. "OK boy....you win....we'll both go." It was noticeably easier to get the big dog in the front seat of his truck after less than a week of Doc Carlin's "miracle cure".

At first glance, it seemed there was nothing special about the balance of background checks that Gerry faxed to him since he received that first batch a couple of days ago. Muldoon was just surprised at the volume. He didn't object because these comparatively easy tasks were definite money makers for his mushrooming career of a private investigator. It was approaching 11:00 pm before Muldoon got down to the last couple of remaining checks. It while running up information on them that something caught his eye.

Both of the last two applicants showed up as having some prior employment history with Grevyev Co., Inc. LLC. Muldoon knew all too well that "Grevyev" was nothing more than a spin on the first name of his old adversary Yevgrev Andreovitch. The blood thirsty Russian ran a lot of his frauds through his Grevyev Co. He had a pyramid of shell companies through which he squeezed his ill-gotten gains in and out and all around before he spun them out to off-shore set ups in the Caymans and Mauritius.

Muldoon spent the last four of his seven years on the Fraud Unit trying to nail Andreovitch. And nail him he did. It took enormous hours of painstaking, detailed work to "connect the dots" on the high living and footloose Russian, but Muldoon and his staff nailed him. It was a great way to end his twenty years on the force.

What seemed odd to Muldoon was why anybody who cozied up with Andreovitch or *any* of his companies wouldn't worry about it showing up on a basic background or credit check. "There's no way Gerry will recommend either of these guys for employ-ment. I wonder what company they're applying to." Muldoon said to the resting Mugsy, who had no opinion on the matter. But it was strange that *two* former employees of Grevyev Co. would be applying for jobs at the same time and wind up in requests for background checks through Gerry's reputable security firm. "I'll just fax the findings back to him but ask him in person on Sunday." Muldoon did not want to raise sensitive issues via the fax. "Better to save it for our private conversation."

It was midnight by the time Muldoon got Mugsy home and settled in for the night. He flopped onto his comfy couch and began to make a list of the kinds of questions he wanted to ask Kitty's son, Patrick, on Saturday. "Kids are always more inclined to spill out information if they aren't being stared down by their parents -- did you know that Mugsy?" The fast-healing Irish wolfhound was fast asleep on his own cushy mattress next to the fireplace. Muldoon just smiled at the sleeping hound "Some partner *you* are!"

He knew that seventeen-year old Patrick would have a take on his friend Paul Skudnick's unusual death that he'd never get from Paul's mother Wanda…..or for that matter from Patrick's mother. "He'll give me information on this Esperanza girlfriend. Teenage boys always talk to their best friends about girlfriends…..a lot of them boast too much" he said "and some of them boast when there is nothing to boast about. It never fails. I want to find out which category Paul Skutnick falls into."

With a full day behind him, Muldoon got up and turned off the downstairs lights. He had another look at Mugsy before he started to climb the stairs up to his bedroom.

"Hey Mugsy" he whispered "anybody ever tell you that you snore?!"

It wasn't long before Muldoon was in bed throwing out a few loud zzz's of his own.

Tomorrow would be another day for Muldoon and Mugsy.

Chapter Twelve

Frettyman Lake was at its most beautiful early in the morning. It was Muldoon's favorite time to sit on the back deck with a cup of his favorite black coffee and reflect on his good fortune. When he returned from his globetrotting travels, he spurned many lucrative offers for this and that from friends and colleagues in the big city. He felt lucky enough to still be held in enough high regard to be offered as many jobs as he was, but he knew on the last leg home from California that the big city was no longer for him. It had a vicious way of sucking the life out of a man and if Muldoon learned anything from his two years of traveling, it was that life, indeed ,was too short not to do what you want and too interesting to let it pass you by. While the decision to choose Frettyman Lake as his new home was driven by the memory of fishing with his father, it was sealed by the prospect of having exactly the kind of life he wanted as he entered his 40s. He wanted freedom – financial, professional, personal, sexual and spiritual. "I have very little to prove to anyone anymore" he murmured "and can set my own agenda and challenges."

A lot of people always teased Muldoon about his great luck..... putting his achievements down to the genes of his Irish ancestors. Muldoon knew the real reason for his good fortune was plain old elbow-greased hard work. His charm he often put down to his Irish genes, but his successes he knew were due to his ability to focus on the task at hand, his mountainous sense of ambition and day in and day out relentless determination. That may have resulted in some lucky breaks along the way but Muldoon was pragmatic enough to understand that the breaks came as a result of the bone-crunching hard work. Now he was enjoying the fruits of that labor.

"And who do I share all of them with?!!" he shouted "You!!...you good old dog!" If Mugsy was impressed he didn't show it. He was too busy inspecting the extended lawn, and its various bushes and flower beds that gently sloped to the shore of the lake. There was a 30-foot wooden dock that extended out into the lake to which Muldoon tied his "pride and joy"...an 18-foot hand-made birch bark Indian canoe.....specially outfitted with broad seat panels so Muldoon could row out into the lake and fish to his heart's content.

"This is the life!" he called out to Mugsy, who was standing at the shoreline, beginning to show signs of the stand and lines of the Irish wolfhound's regal bearing once again.

The heavenly solitude of the morning was interrupted when Muldoon heard someone call from around the front of the cabin. "Anyone home?" Muldoon walked around the side of the cabin to see who his visitor might be.

"Hello Doc!" he said as soon as he recognized Mugsy's veterinarian "top of the morning to you!"

"Back at ya!" yelled the Doc "I hope you don't mind me coming out unexpectedly but I have a light schedule today and was anxious to have a look at Mugsy."

"Not at all.....come on in. Have you had any breakfast yet?"

"Just coffee....and bad coffee from the diner at that!"

"Let's go into the kitchen. I have great coffee and I'll fix us up a proper Irish breakfast."

"I won't say no to that" said Doc warmly.

Before Doc took a seat at the table he took a couple of minutes to observe Mugsy meandering in the back yard. He was very pleased with what he saw. "He's doing better than I had hoped, Muldoon. You're obviously taking very good care of him."

"Mugsy has a real will to survive, Doc. In saw it in him when I first laid eyes on him in the pound. Do you want me to call him in for you?"

"No…just let him roam around as he is. I want to watch his movements. They will tell me a lot."

Muldoon started to pull all the fixin's for an Irish breakfast out of the fridge: the rashers, black and white pudding, tomatoes and the special Irish sausage. "How are scrambled eggs for you, Doc?"

"Whatever's easy." he responded "where'd you learn to cook like this anyway?"

"Oh…here and there and everywhere along the way. I find it relaxing."

"Crimeny" laughed Doc "I'm 70 years old and my specialty is soup from a can."

"I can teach you how to make soup, Doc. It's easier than pouring a glass of water. You can make a big batch of your favorite kind and then freeze it….it's better for you than all the salt in that canned soup from the grocery store."

"My old habits are probably too hard to break at this stage….. but I'll think about the cooking lesson later." declared Doc "but I have to tell you, this is some excellent coffee you have here."

"Let me give you a little refill" said Muldoon as he reached for the coffee pot.

"Don't get me used to this!" cracked Doc "I'm likely to be knocking on your door every morning!"

Doc raised his coffee mug in mock salute to his gracious host.

After they finished the superb Irish breakfast Doc said "Let's have a good look at your pal, Mugsy, now."

The aging but very wise veterinarian was very pleased with his close inspection and wrote down two new vitamin supplements for Muldoon to add to Mugsy's "three squares" and suggested that he begin the new regime on Sunday. Muldoon reminded Doc that he'd be in the big city almost all of Sunday. "Who's going to take care of Mugsy while you are gone?" asked Doc.

"I thought I'd see if Kitty's son, Patrick, wouldn't mind. I'll pay him of course. I can drive him out here in the morning and he can have the run of the cabin for the day."

Doc agreed that Patrick was a good choice. "He's been working at the pound since he was a kid. I've watched him over the years and he has a real easy way with animals. If you leave the new supplements out and instructions on how to administer him, I'm sure Patrick will get the job done. If you want, I'll come out 'round mid-afternoon and see how he's doing."

"I wouldn't mind that at all Doc but I don't want to put you to any trouble. If you say Patrick is reliable, that's good enough for me."

"No trouble at all" replied Doc "I am all about an animal's well being….dedicated my life to it after all!!"

"OK…. I'll set it up with Patrick when I talk to him tomorrow at the parking lot."

"Big pow-wow in the parking lot?" teased Doc

"Not really…..I just want to talk to him about this Skudnick kid who died. Patrick's mother told me they were really good pals. I want to get his perspective on the whole thing."

"The whole thing's a tragedy from beginning to end, if you ask me."

"How so?" asked Muldoon

"Paul was a good kid…..surprisingly so…considering the lousy home environment he had…..the kid had some real potential."

"I heard all about the loser father he had."

"Yep. Pretty much all around useless. My brother-in-law was the high school football coach when Wally was trying out for the team twenty-five years ago. He cut him from the squad for having a lazy attitude and then Wally turns around any sets fire to the equipment room. Of course, the DA couldn't make the case stick, but everybody knew it was Wally. He had the markings of an alcoholic before he graduated high school. Nobody knows why Wanda married him. He used them both….Wanda and the kid….as punching bags for a long time."

"What about drugs….does anybody know if he used them or kept them around the house?"

"Wouldn't surprise me…..but I can't say for sure. I always tried to keep my distance from Wally……especially in The Belly Up….he could be a mean drunk. If he was popping pills or doing anything else, I never saw it. You'd be barking up the wrong tree, if you don't mind my canine pun, Muldoon, if you think Paul Skudnick was fooling around with drugs. He just was _not_ the type" Doc said adamantly "that's what makes this whole incident such a tragedy…nobody can figure it out."

"Are drugs a big thing in this town?"

Doc shook his head sadly. "Never used to be….but over the past couple of years, they seem to have slid their way in here. It's a real pity."

"Why would Chief Branderford tell anyone that Paul was a known "druggie"…..nothing so far seems to point to that. But, that's what Barry the Gambler told everyone in The Belly Up."

"Well, first of all Muldoon, always….and I do mean _always_…. take whatever Barry the Gambler says with a grain of salt…and a rather large grain at that…..especially if he's making one of his "announcements" in The Belly Up. And second of all…don't get me started on that sorry sack of a Police Chief we have here now."

Muldoon was dumbfounded. Again, as with Wanda, he did not say anything about the fact that Peter was his partner in the big city but it was twice now in the past two days that he heard disparaging remarks about him.

"I take it you are not fond of the Chief." said Muldoon

"I just don't think he does the job he supposed to do, that's all. We had a perfectly capable and respectable Chief......Nick Spalata was his name......and all of sudden about two and a half years ago he gets replaced by Branderford. Spalata gets put out to pasture. "Early retirement" is what the newspaper called it and Branderford is in......and, as I see it, is not responsive to the needs of the town."

"What happened to Mr. Spalata?"

Doc pointed out the window. "He lives way out there -- on the far end of the lake. Almost never comes into town."

Chapter Thirteen

It was barely 9:30 am when Muldoon pulled into the parking lot next to the German Meat Market. He gave Patrick a wave from the driver's seat. After a nice lazy Friday afternoon in the cabin watching "Lawrence of Arabia" on dvd for the umpteenth time, Muldoon wanted to get productive today and put all his ducks in a row before he flew down to the big city tomorrow.

"'Morning Mr. Frickey" said Patrick as Muldoon pulled his truck safely into one of the available spaces "that truck gets better looking every time I see it!"

"Maybe someday.....someday...I'll let you have a spin in it" Muldoon jested "how are you this fine morning anyway?" Patrick gave an assured nod to indicate that all was well. "Have you got a minute for me?" he asked the teenager. Again Patrick nodded. "My mother said you wanted to have a word."

Muldoon advised Patrick that he didn't have to talk about his best friend's death if was too uncomfortable "but it surely would help me help Paul's mother figure some of this out" he added.

"Not to worry, Mr. Frickey. I'll help anyway I can. I miss Paul something awful but there is nothing I can do to bring him back so I just have to accept it -- accept the fact that he's dead. I don't have to accept the way he died."

"It bothers you, then, that he died using drugs?"

"Definitely that. But it pisses me off that the last one to be with him while he was alive was that skank, Esperanza."

"You didn't like her? I mean, she died too, you know…she was only sixteen."

"It was no loss to me. She was a skank -- been giving it away to every dog in the street since she was fifteen. Everybody knew it."

"What was Paul doing with her – aside from the obvious."

"That's just it, Mr. Frickey…..Paul wasn't doing it with her….. with nobody, if you want the truth."

"The truth always helps" said Muldoon.

"The night he died was the first night he was going to do "the obvious" as you say. Pauly had it all planned out. His mom was working a double shift and wouldn't be home until 1:00 am. Esperanza was supposed to meet him at his house at 7:00 pm – jump into horizontal – and be clear of the place by 9:00."

"Paul was a virgin?"

"Yep…no crime in it, I mean, but he wanted to lose it bad…. but he was always a little on the shy side where that's concerned."

Muldoon probed a little further. "He was a confident student…..confident athlete…..well liked…handsome young kid….. what was the problem?"

"He had lots going for him" explained Patrick " but he had a few self-esteem issues…..his old man used to dog him something awful when he was a kid….beat him blue sometimes, too."

Muldoon acknowledged that he knew all about Wally's violent tendencies. "But that doesn't explain why a nice kid like Paul would have anything to do with a sixteen-year old girl with a torrid reputation. Why not a girl from his own high school for his first time?"

"There were plenty who were interested, believe me. They used to come up to me all the time and ask for his cell number, but Pauly could never seal the deal. Besides, this Esperanza chick practically stalked him!"

"How so?"

"We had a wrestling match about two months ago over at her high school --- it's on the outskirts of town -- lousy neighborhood and not very safe. Anyway, we mauled them on the mat.... they were no match for us. Pauly had one of his best matches that day and the crowd was really behind him.....and believe me, Mr. Frickey....it was not lost on any of the girls how great Pauly looked in his wrestling gear....they all gave him the eye, trust me."

"How did Esperanza figure into this?"

"She was there...in the stands with some of her girlfriends. She was whooping wildly for Pauly which struck me a bit strange..... her so obviously rooting against her own high school team.... but then me and some of the other guys just figured it was just another girl who was hot for him."

"Paul never paid her any mind?" said Muldoon continuing his questioning

"Well....I won't say that he didn't look at her a few times.....I mean for sixteen years old she had *some* figure on her."

"He never talked to her?"

"Talk!!! Are you kidding? He never got a chance!"

Muldoon was confused. "What do you mean?'

"I swear I don't know how she did this....but after the match we were all in the locker room....changing and showering and generally strutting around celebrating our victory. And....in she walks with a huge armful of towels....walks over to Pauly's locker...drops the towels on the bench...lifts her T-shirt and says 'These are yours anytime you want them!'......Incredible....I saw four guys make a dash into the showers for a cold one!"

"What was Paul's reaction?"

"He just shrugged and watched her run out of the gym locker.....she was bold as brass, that one."

"And after the match?.....the stalking, as you say...when did that start?"

"Next day" said Patrick matter-of-factly "she started phoning his home telephone – basically it was his Mom's telephone, an old fashioned land line. She probably got the number from the phone book. She was calling it two and three times a night. Mrs. Skudnick started to get annoyed and believe me it took a lot to get under Pauly's mother's skin...she's a really, really nice lady. But she didn't like the notion of this strange girl invading her home space....and she let Pauly know it, too."

"How long did this go on?" asked Muldoon

"After about two weeks Pauly broke down and agreed to meet her after school."

"Here in town?"

"Yeah...he told her that if she really wanted to see him, she'd have to get over here. They met at the diner."

"How did that go?"

"Pauly told me that he was going to tell her to flake off...stop calling the house...get a life....you know, that sort of thing.....he thought it was getting ridiculous."

"Let me guess" interrupted Muldoon "Pauly, wanting so badly to pop his cherry, fell into a weakened state when Esperanza started to bat her eyelashes at him....right?"

"Eyelashes nothing! Pauly told me later that she shows up wearing a see-through blouse and no bra....and in the middle of eating his hamburger, she tells him that she not wearing any underwear under her skirt and that he can have her right out in the back of the diner if he wanted."

"And she's sixteen years old?"

"A sixteen- year old skank – like I told you."

Muldoon was beginning to think that this whole tragic incident was nothing more than raging teenage hormones gone wild until Patrick finished the rest of his story.

He told Muldoon that Esperanza started showing up at their high school at the end of the day looking for Paul. "She had to have been cutting classes at her own school to get all the way over here to ours by closing bell."

Patrick also said that once in a while Paul would make small talk with her, but no serious ovations for a date. "Some of the guys told Pauly to bang her and get it over with.....maybe she'd go away."

Muldoon made the comment that it seemed like Paul was letting it drag on too long to his own detriment.

"Pauly knew that he was better than this Esperanza lunatic. He told me so lots of times but he didn't want to just do her and then throw her for road kill."

"If the stalking was getting ridiculous, as you say, why didn't Paul or Mrs. Skudnick report it to the police?"

"He didn't want to look like a sissy...like he couldn't handle a shrimpy sixteen-year old girl. Besides, Chief Branderford marked him the very first day he saw the two of them eating at the diner. Drugs are big time and easy to get over in her neighborhood and he got a "guilt by association" thing from Branderford, who will use any excuse to rope the kids here in for any trumped up offense."

"I'm getting the feeling that not too many people like Chief Branderford" stated Muldoon.

"I know that nobody my age likes him....that's for sure."

"Did Paul talk to you about the set-up the night he died?" Patrick nodded.

"He told me he was going to finally do it because he was sick of her pestering him. I told him to go ahead and do the deed and be done with it."

"Did he mention anything about drugs?.....anything at all?"

"No, sir" said Patrick "nothing. After he told me what the

plan was all he did was ask me for some condoms."

"And you were able to oblige your pal, no doubt?" said Muldoon wryly

Patrick looked at him at just said "I was never as shy as Pauly."

"So it must have been Esperanza who brought the ecstasy that night?" asked Muldoon

"I have no doubt of it, Mr. Frickey.....not a doubt in my mind."

"And she got it from?"

Patrick just shrugged his shoulders. "I don't know....could have been a lot of places over where she lived.....but she's dead.... Pauly's dead....so how will anyone ever find out? It's a mess."

"Maybe not" said Muldoon "maybe not....I'll just keep digging. But you've been very helpful, Patrick. Thanks."

"No problem, Mr. Frickey....anytime."

As Muldoon turned to walk away Patrick added "Umm...Mr. Frickey...this was a *private* conversation wasn't it?....if you get my drift" he said nodding his head toward the dog pound where his mother worked.

"It was definitely private, Patrick. Don't worry about it. That privacy factor, though, works both ways, you know. Mums the word."

"You got it!" replied the teenager with a smile.

"Keep an eye on my truck....I want to pop in the market here and get some of those smoked pork chops." Muldoon took a couple more strides towards the market and turned back. "Say, Patrick... are you available to take care of Mugsy on Sunday....say from about 11:00 am until 5 or 6? I'll pay you ten bucks an hour."

"Ten bucks and hour!! I am TOTALLY available! Totally!!" screamed the teenager.

"OK....I'll pick you up at your house at 10:30 am on Sunday."

Chapter Fourteen

Smoked pork chops in hand as well as two whole cut-up chickens, three pounds of lean ground beef and four rib eye steaks, and a half pound of salami and a pound of sliced roast beef thrown in for good measure, Muldoon sauntered out of the German Meat Market with a "I am nothing if not a meat eater" smile on his face. "And top quality stuff, too." His naturally lean, muscled physique was not often enough supplemented by a regular course of fruits and vegetables, as a priority, unless he was in the mood. Today he was both in the mood and in luck.

There was a young man setting up a fruit and vegetable stand on the sidewalk a few feet from the entrance to the parking lot. Muldoon had not seen him there before and he was carting the fresh goods from the back of his pick-up truck coincidentally parked near Muldoon's. Patrick was giving the "fruit and veg" vendor a hand with unloading his wares. He saw the heavy loaded bag that Muldoon was carrying and laughed "Hey, Mr. Frickey…I thought you were going in for just a couple of pork chops!"

"I couldn't resist" replied Muldoon "that place is a carnivore's delight."

"How 'bout something to balance out all that meat? A little something from my stand here to give your heart arteries a break!" chirped in the fruit and veg guy.

Muldoon knew he was right and started to head for the stand. "Oh....Mr. Frickey...this is my friend, Lou.....this is his fruit and veg stand." said Patrick by way of introduction.

"Pleased to meet you, Lou" said Muldoon as they shook hands "what do you recommend?"

"Just about anything on this stand, Mr. Frickey to counter what looks to me to be about 15-20 pounds of meat your carrying there!"

Lou guessed correctly that Muldoon was "not much of a salad man" who thought lettuce should lie at the bottom of a rabbit cage and nowhere else. With his work (or selling techniques) cut out for him he convinced Muldoon to skip the iceberg lettuce and take a chance on the romain. He explained that nothing could be easier than ripping off a couple of leaves of it, "wash 'em, lay 'em out on a small plate and slice a tomato and half a cucumber onto it. A little salt and pepper and you're good to go! Easy as pie." He added that Muldoon's heart would be eternally grateful and he'd still have room in his stomach for a nice big steak.

"There's twenty other ways to make that combination interesting but I think you should start out with the simple stuff or you'll probably wind up retreating to a bag of packaged potato chips with your steak.....am I right?" Muldoon nodded sheepishly.

"Are you some kind of chef or something, Lou?"

"Naw... this is just a business for me....a way to make some money. I'm actually studying to be a plumber. I have my stand out on Saturdays and Sundays during the day and I get my on-the-job apprentice training during the week. I've been doing it since I left high school and I'm almost ready for the written exam."

While Lou was telling Muldoon about his future plans, Patrick was loading up a few bags of grapes, cherries, mangoes and a half dozen oranges. "Here Mr. Frickey....you need these, too......don't want your teeth to fall out!" he joked. As if that would ever happen. Muldoon Frickey had a pair of the whitest, straightest, full mouth of perfect teeth this side of Paul Newman. They were the color of pure snow. He took the bags of fruit from Patrick and glibly told Lou to "Ring me up."

"Are you here every weekend?" asked Muldoon. In a slightly exasperated tone Lou said that this was his first weekend at the parking lot. It was a prime location and Lou had trouble getting a permit to put his stand there. Muldoon agreed that it was a great spot – good for Lou and conveniently located for potential customers. "Good for everybody. Who could be against that?"

"Branderford" snarled Lou "that Barney Fife knock-off . He tried to squash my permit application. His ploy didn't work and that really pissed him off something bad....because I essentially pushed him aside."

Muldoon was getting a bad feeling inside but kept it to himself. He asked Lou rather casually "Why would the Chief of Police bother about a license permit for a fruit and veg stand?"

Lou told Muldoon that two years ago when Branderford was still pretty new on the job, he tried to "tattoo me with a drug selling rap. I don't touch the stuff – never have – but he was relentless. I confronted him one day and told him he didn't intimdate me one bit...that if he thought he was going to scare me into pleading guilty he was dead wrong. I was one year out of high school and well into my apprenticeship training. I told him that if he wanted to unstrap the gun belt we could step behind the abandon tire factory and I'd knock his teeth down his throat."

"Threatening a police officer, Chief or not Lou, is never a good idea." advised Muldoon

"Don't get me wrong, Mr. Frickey....I'm a law abiding guy, but these were extreme circumstances...he was putting my ability to get my plumber's license in jeopardy. Besides, there was nobody there when I said it and it was only going to me my word against his. He was sitting in his squad car and he knew I meant what I said. I told him he was going to choke to death on his own pearly whites."

"What happened?"

"He told the DA to drop the charges when he found out that my uncle was the County judge. He knew he had no case to begin with and he knew for certain that I didn't give a shit if he was the Chief of Police or the Queen of Sheba! I told him in no uncertain terms that I do not *ever* allow anybody to bully me and he was just not used to any teenagers in this town standing up to him like that."

Lou looked like he could hold his own, too. He was six feet tall and about as buffed a plumber-in-training that this small town had. He was not afraid to show it off either with his sleeveless T-shirt and enviable washboard abs. Tall, dark, handsome and tough…..not surprising, then, to Muldoon that Peter backed away. It was reminiscent of how their snitches in the big city reacted when Peter got too rough with them. Muldoon remembered time after time trying to convince Peter that bullying almost never works……temporarily maybe, but in the long run it always comes back to bite you in the ass. That never completely sunk in with Peter.

"That was two years ago, Lou. I'm guessing that you're about twenty-one years old now – no longer a teenager. Why do you think the Chief is still trying to throw a spanner into your works?"

"Because he's a petty SOB that's why. He gives me the evil eye whenever he drives by and I give it right back to him, too…gave him the finger last year when my stand was ten blocks down the street…next to the Western Union office…and practically dared him to stop the car and get out…..of course he kept right on driving. He complained to the Permit Board last week that having my stand here on the sidewalk next to the parking lot would inhibit traffic flow. It was a joker's argument and the Board gave me my permit in spite of what he said. When he left the hearing he turns to me in the hallway and says 'I still got my eye on you.' I says right back 'Fuck you Barney Fife....I got *my eye* on you!"

Muldoon wanted to ratchet down the vitriol somewhat and disarmingly asked Lou "You probably get to see a lot on these streets with your stand out all weekend long, don't you?'

"I see plenty, Mr. Frickey...and know plenty, too. I'm born and raised here and will probably die here, too. This is my home town."

"And" Muldoon suggested "you might notice any strange comings and goings...stuff out of the ordinary?"

"Yep" replied Lou.....on *and* off the job."

"Ever go in to The Belly Up?"

"Like almost every Saturday night! You'll find me in there letting off some steam with my pals. Saturday nights everybody in The Belly Up is looking for a little action – if you know what I mean."

"Loud and crowded, is it?"

"Without fail" Lou told him "especially on karaoke nights. They have that every other week or so....place goes nuts."

"Sounds like a lot of fun."

"It can be until fools like me take the mike and try to sing anything!" Lou smiled "why do you ask?"

He told Lou about looking into the death of Paul Skudnick.

"What a pity" said Lou "I knew Paul...and Patrick here,too.....since they were in grade school. They were freshman in high school when I was a senior. It's an awful thing for poor Mrs. Skudnick."

"And the girl?"

"She wasn't from this part of town....didn't know her....but I do a considerable amount of apprentice plumbing work over in her area....bleeding old radiators in tenement buildings...stuff like that."

"Have you heard anything about her death over there?"

"Not yet." admitted Lou

"Well, keep your ear to the ground...and on Saturday nights in The Belly Up....if you can still see straight...keep your eyes open for me, OK? If you see or hear anything useful, I'll make it worth your while."

Lou agreed. "And" said Muldoon in parting "both of you.... keep all this under your hat. Deal?"

Both Lou and Patrick said "It's a deal."

Chapter Fifteen

There was no reason that Muldoon could think of *not* to stop in The Belly Up for a cold Sam Adams and a brief chat with Teddy. After he unloaded his bags of meat, fruit and veggies in his truck, he dashed across the street for a bit of small town socializing.

Teddy, as he always was on Saturday afternoon, was happily saddled behind the bar encouraging his patrons to dig deep into their pockets for beer money and deeper in for tip money. "I don't stand here all day long because any of you mugs are so pretty!!.... especially you Carl!" he said teasing his favorite customer.

"You want a tip?" Carl droned "Then get over to that jukebox and play me some Johnny Cash....no..no....not Cash...I changed my mind...today I feel like listening to the beautiful voice of Eddy Arnold."

"Carl...come over here with me. I am going to teach you how to operate this juke."

"I told you before...I don't want to learn...just play me my music...here's five dollars....load me up on Eddy!!"

As Muldoon pulled out a bar stool near the front window he piped in on the never-ending jukebox argument between Teddy and Carl. "What's with all this Eddy Arnold....he's worse than Al Jolson" he said trying to get a rise out of Carl.

"Teddy...that's a great idea....play me some Al Jolson, too!.....

great idea, pal…None better than Al Jolson, is there?"

Muldoon saw at least two empty vodka glasses sitting in front of Carl and he was working on a third. One more and Johnny Cash and Al Jolson were going to start to sound the same to Carl.

"Hiya Muldoon" said Teddy as he strode back to his position of dominance behind the bar "how's things in your world?"

"Can't complain."

"Good to see you back in mine.…..you're a welcome relief to the rolling thunder of insanity we have in here on a regular basis."

Muldoon took a few deep gulps from his bottle of Sam Adams and surveyed the crowd. Carl, of course, was there holding court at dead center. Two guys from the local electricians union were seated in between Muldoon and Carl, moaning over possible union layoffs. There were two passably pretty girls nursing glasses of white wine down the bar from Carl. They looked like they were camped out with cell phones, compacts, purses, cigarettes and lighters carefully arranged around their wine glasses. Muldoon thought their silver-colored fingernails were long enough to be registered as deadly weapons. Two seats down from the girls was a man who looked like he had spent his last dime on the "Quick Pick" electronic numbers game hanging above the row of whiskey bottles behind the bar. His ripped up tickets were all over the bar in front of him but no signs of the piles of dough he probably had his heart set on when he first sat down. Everybody who lost at the game somehow always thought there was a "promise of winning" in the next game. Everybody who never bothered with the $1 ticket to play called it "video crack".

At the far end of the bar, sitting alone, as usual, looking like he just made a pact with the devil was the gloomy presence of Larry Lutursky.…tapping on the bar with his empty shot glass, indicating that he wanted a refill.……the louder the tap, the more he needed the shot.

After he sated Larry's urgent need, Teddy sat in the bartender's stool on the inside of the bar up near Muldoon and started to ask him if he'd made his move on Patti-cake yet.

"You have a one-track mind, Teddy" joked Muldoon "but to answer your question…sort of."

"Well, 'sort of' is better than not doing anything…..what's the delay?"

"I've been pre-occupied…business things, you know."

"Anything interesting?"

Testing a relative stranger and pumping him for information were delicate sides of the coin and Muldoon wanted to test Teddy first.

"Can you keep things mum…I mean are you any good at keeping information close to your chest?"

"Just try me, man….I'd be the best prisoner of war ever…. name rank and serial number only." the twenty-five-year old bartender proudly stated.

Muldoon started to tell Teddy about his involvement in the Skudnick case. "Everybody feels bad for Wanda" interrupted Teddy almost immediately. "She was so freaking proud of that kid. They both seemed to come into their own after she dumped that mongrel she married."

"Wally…right?"

"That's the mongrel I mean".

"You know him?"

"The first week I was on the job here ….two years ago…..he came in rotten drunk and cursing his wife something awful….. said he was going to kill her for divorcing him….the rest of the customers were getting embarrassed by his foul language. So, I told him to quiet down or he was going to have to leave."

"That have any effect on him."

"It was like talking to a wall. So, I ordered him out. I told him as long as I was on bar, he was banned from The Belly Up."

"Did *that* have any effect on him?"

"He took a swing at me and I grabbed the little mongrel by the back of his shirt and tossed him out the front door."

"Pretty effective maneuver…..did it stick?'

"I think he's been in here during some of the other bartenders' shifts, but he tried to come in the next week when I was on and I never said a thing to him…..just pointed at the front door."

"And….?"

"He left……and hasn't been back on *my* shift since."

"This kid's not very big but he sure doesn't seem like he's afraid of much" Muldoon thought to himself as he watched Teddy re-fill the passably pretty girls' wine glasses ….on the house. "Got some charm to him, too."

Teddy sat down near Muldoon again and said "That's Eleanor and Alice down there at towards the end of the bar……always reliable, if you know what I mean."

The girls waved to Muldoon and he smiled back…..sort of.

"You ever hang out here when you're not tending bar, Teddy?"

"Yeah….lots of times….I get along pretty well with the rest of the bartenders…well, there's one I don't like ….but nobody likes her anyway…she has a tendency to let underage kids in here…… drives Pietro nutty."

"He should hire a bouncer…somebody to check ID's at the door."

"It takes no time and hardly any money to get a good fake ID…..you must have seen a lot of them when you were on the force." Muldoon nodded. He knew that if young kids wanted to drink, they'd always find a way.

"What's the night crowd like?"

"Depends" replied Teddy "different nights draw different

crowds….some bartenders have their own following."

"Like the one who gives underage kids a pass?"

"Yep…..they know they can't get in on my shift….so they try others."

"What night does she work?"

"Tuesdays…….there's always a few high schoolers playing hookey on Wednesday from too much nooky and booze on Tuesday night."

"Have you ever been in here on Tuesdays?"

"Sure…plenty of times….don't get me wrong…the place is not over-run with minors…..but there's more than a few who slip in and out during the course of the evening."

Muldoon took the last few swigs of his beer and looked Teddy straight in the eyes. "Ever see Paul Skudnick in here on one of those Tuesday nights?"

Teddy kind of felt like he was trapped. "I won't lie, Muldoon….I saw him in here once….just once….about a year ago but I didn't see him drinking….some of the wrestling team came in and they were celebrating a big win over a rival team in the next county."

"Just the once?"

"That's all I ever saw…. I swear."

"What about the girl who died with him?"

"I don't know anything about her. Some guys from her neighborhood come in sometimes, but it seems like they are always getting into fights out back."

"Anybody ever call the cops?"

"Nah….they're just bar fights…nothing big….not like gangs or anything….they usually break up after a few hard punches."

Just then Carl was getting antsy again and shouted "Hey, Teddy….lemme hear some more tunes!!"

Muldoon came to the rescue. "Carl……I'll put $5 bucks in for you if you can tell me which actress won the most Oscars ever."

Carl thought for a minute and blurted out "Gloria Swanson!!!....
am I right?...what an actress....lemme tell ya!!"

Muldoon laughed on his way to the jukebox and didn't have
the heart to tell Carl that it was actually Katherine Hepburn.
"You sure do know a lot about actresses, Carl."

"It's my specialty!" replied Carl as he swallowed the last of his
fifth vodka shot.

"Hey, Teddy" said Muldoon "buy the bar on me!! We'll cel-
ebrate Carl's unusual knowledge of movies!"

Carl raised his fist in the air. Eleanor and Alice giggled. The
"Quick Pick" loser was glad to get anything for free. The elec-
tricians shook their heads and said "two shots of tequila, please."
And Larry Lutursky waived the freebie off.

Muldoon moved in for his manipulated closer look. "What's
the matter champ?" he said to Larry "you don't want my booze?
We're just havin' a good time here."

"Don't know you." was Larry's mumbled and snarly reply. And
then he got up and left.

"Now what are you so afraid of?" whispered Muldoon so low
that no one else in the bar heard it.

Muldoon strutted past Carl and gave him a pat on the back
"Gloria Swanson it is!! You're too much Carl, my man."

"Don't give another thought to Larry, Muldoon. He's a very
strange bird. Best part of my day is when he leaves." said Teddy
"he'll come back tonight and be somebody else's problem."

"He's a night time customer, too?"

"Oh, yeah......always.....Larry's a fixture here......actually
more like a barnacle, if you want to know the truth."

Muldoon just shrugged. "Takes all kinds, doesn't it?"

With Teddy tested and pumped, Muldoon decided it was
time to get back to the cabin, have some quality time with Mugsy
and finish preparing for tomorrow's trip to the big city.

Chapter Sixteen

After he picked up Patrick Selarus from his house and brought him out to the cabin to watch over Mugsy for the day, Muldoon drove the eight miles outside the town limit to the hangar where Ken stored his helicopter. Ken was ready and waiting.

"Punctuality and preparation" thought Muldoon as he parked on the side of the hangar "my two favorite attributes." He waved to Ken and said "I hope I haven't kept you waiting."

Ken shook his head. "Nope…..you are exactly on time….very punctual. I got here and hour ago to prep the chopper for our trip."

Ken had already moved the helicopter away from the hangar, gassed it up and was ready to go. "Shall we?" he said to Muldoon as he strutted towards the bird he called "Mysuitisgone".

"What kind of name is that, Ken?…..looks like some foreign word or something" asked Muldoon as he hopped aboard.

"When I retired from the corporate life and commercial airline piloting, I swore I'd never, ever put another suit or uniform on as long as I lived……they can bury me in one, but I won't feel it" he laughed " if you break her name apart it reads 'My-suit-is-gone'…. and believe me, it's gone for good. Haven't worn one in eight years. I only have one left in my closet….save it for funerals!"

"Yeah, I hear you….I wore a police uniform for thirteen years and a shirt and tie for the next seven while I was investigating fraud.......I'll still wear a suit, tho.....but you had better give me a *real* good reason to do so!!"

As the copter rose into the sky, Muldoon marveled at the beauty of its plush inside. "This is luxury travelling, isn't it?"

"It's a real pleasure to fly her" replied Ken "and hardly ever any shortage of passengers, either.....luxurious *and* lucrative!"

"That surprises me.....I wouldn't figure that there'd be anybody flying down to the big city from this small town with any regularity."

"Oh....I get them from all over Belleva County.....not just here. Although, I do take Chief Branderford down to the big city maybe two or three times a month....always down and back in the same day......always for the same reason."

"What's that?" asked Muldoon

"Says he's going down to visit his wife and kids......says that when his kids are finished high school, his wife is going to move up here with him permanent-like."

That statement did not square with Muldoon Frickey:Private Investigator but he let it drop. He saw no reason to raise an issue with Ken. Obviously, Muldoon was the only other person in town, other than Peter himself, who knew the truth about the long-standing ,withering state of his marriage to Jennie.

He just simply changed the subject. "What's our flight time, Ken?"

"Should be about 35-40 minutes. We have a nice, easy wind and the best part......no traffic!" he jested. Ken clearly was a happy man in the air....like he was born to fly.

A short time into their flight Muldoon decided to ask Ken what he knew about the Skudnick family. He thought he might have an insight others might not inasmuch as he professed to know everybody in the small town.

"Wally was a hell-raiser from an early age" said Ken "pretty much an all-around embarrassment to his family. His parents were immigrants from Poland after World War II and didn't speak a lot of English -- never really could master the language but they both worked like mules to put together a home. Wally was just always a bad seed. He was in reform school by the time he was eleven and stayed there for two years. From my way of thinking the only thing that changed about him after he came out was that he was even more determined to raise hell. His old man finally tossed him out of the house for good when he was sixteen."

"Where are his parents now?" asked Muldoon

"Dead....both of them. I think it's ten or twelve years by now. They died within a month of each other. Nice couple, actually....church-goers and all.....I think they couldn't live without one another. So, nobody expected Mr. Skudnick to live very long after his wife died....and sure enough, one month later they were burying him right next to her."

"Did Wally get the house....or anything like that?"

"Like I said....all Wally got was a boot in the ass out of the house by the time he was sixteen...and it was exactly what he deserved, if you ask me. No....the proceeds from the sale of the house and effects were given to their local church by terms of a will....nothing for the reprobate son."

"Why on earth did Wanda marry him.....was she pregnant?"

"No.....not pregnant. Not Wanda......she was not that kind of girl."

"Then why?"

"Ah....who knows?......who knows why women do the things they do....I sure don't....do you?"

"No....not really, I suppose" Muldoon said with an air of resignation.

The approach and landing at the big city's heliport was as

smooth as silk. Muldoon confirmed the 5:00 pm departure time with Ken and asked him in passing what he was going to do all day. "Beat the pants off Kevin over there – the heliport manager – in game after game of gin rummy. We never play for very high stakes, but I love to win and Kevin hates to lose so he keeps coming back for more!" Ken said with a hearty laugh.

Muldoon smiled, waved goodbye and headed towards the taxi stand and his meeting with Gerry Dowling.

Chapter Seventeen

The taxi ride into the midtown heart of the big city made Muldoon realize how happy he was *not* to be living there anymore…..how happy he actually was to be settled in on Frettyman Lake. "How did I ever survive this rat race for twenty years, I'll never know." he mused

In his heart he knew the answer. Muldoon Frickey was a born and bred big city boy. He grew up there, went to grade school and high school and graduated from the police academy in the big city. He watched his parents go to work every day in the big city and spent twenty years on the force doing exactly the same. It was in his blood. But when he retired, he decided to "get out while the gettin' was good" and he never looked back or questioned his decision.

So, he was not at all envious when he stepped off the elevator on the 53rd floor into the lobby of The Revona Group International /Security Consultants. Almost anyone else may have had a twinge of jealousy because the view of the big city below was simply breathtaking and the décor of the lobby was all dark wood, thick carpeting, elegant and plush furniture and a most attractive receptionist. It looked like the interior of a very exclusive private club.

The greeting he received from the receptionist was a far cry from the one Patti-cake gave him at The Belly Up but Muldoon secretly knew he preferred the latter.

She invited Muldoon to sit down and advised that "Mr. Dowling's secretary, Miss Rainer will be with you directly."

Sure enough, less than a minute later, Louise Rainer walked through the door that led to the interior offices and introduced herself.

"Let me escort you back to Mr. Dowling's private conference room, Muldoon. He's waiting for you."

The office hallways were wide enough for Muldoon and Louise to walk side by side. It was rare that he ever had seen a woman so self-possessed, professional and downright sexy at the same time....seamed nylons on too, he noticed "That's gotta drive Gerry to distraction!" It made him think for a second that maybe...just maybe he'd been away from the big city too long. But then he thought of Patti-cake and realized where his true desires lie.

Louise rapped lightly on the conference room door and showed Muldoon in and turned to make her exit back to her own office, just outside Gerry's.

The two former colleagues greeted each other warmly. "Your world travels have done wonders for that baby face of yours, Muldoon......put a bit of age on it!" he teased.

"And you look like you've got somebody shopping for your clothes nowdays.....Brooks Brothers, am I right?....how'd you graduate from the "All men/all sizes" suit rack to Brooks Brothers in two years!!" quipped Muldoon "Christ.....and fancy cuff links, to boot. I think I'd better sit down before I fall down!"

Gerry laughed at the more-correct-than-he-wanted-to-remember reference to his previously frumpy wardrobe. "I have to look the part, man!! And, it could all be yours....all you have to do is say the word. I'll take you on starting tomorrow morning. You're the best fraud investigator I ever knew."

Muldoon just shook his head.

"Seriously, Muldoon…..what the hell are doing up there on Prettyman Lake?"

"Um….Ger… it's Frettyman Lake….not Prettyman."

"Yeah….whatever you want to call it….come back to reality man…..there's huge money here just waiting for you."

"I had plenty of reality on the force for twenty years, thank you very much." said Muldoon without regret "but I'm grateful for the bones you are throwing me to get my business started."

"No problem…there's plenty more where that came from" said Gerry knowing full well that he was going nowhere with offers of full-time employment for Muldoon "besides you are making me look good to the client with the accuracy and speed of your work."

Muldoon smiled again "Hmmm…..some things never change do they?"

Gerry nodded and wryly replied "The past is the past, buddy……this is now….and we have a problem."

"I haven't got a problem in the world, Gerry…..I'm livin' the Life of Riley! What did you want to see me for with such urgency anyway?"

"Just what I said…

"What are you talking about?"

"The problem, Muldoon……I think you've got a problem up there in paradise."

Muldoon's smile disappeared.

Gerry launched into a long, detailed explanation of how the case against Yevgrev Andreovitch fell apart about a month after Muldoon retired, left town and headed out to travel to parts unknown leaving no contact as he followed the rattle of his gypsy bones from city to city around the world.

"Nobody knew how to get a hold of you…nobody knew where

you were. The plea deal with the DA collapsed when Yevgrev's legal team said they had a dirty cop on the string for a year. This cop compromised every bit of important evidence that you and your team put together."

"Are you telling me that some cop from the force was on that Russian's payroll?"

"Yeah….and was on it *big time*, let me tell you" Gerry reported "and every bit of tainted evidence was tossed out. Kaput!"

Muldoon had his head in his hands and could barely believe what he was hearing. The Yevgrev Andreovitch case was his shining hour. He worked it with remarkable precision and took great pride that the black-hearted Russian was probably going to do 20-25 years in the Big House.

"What happened……didn't Yevgrev get any time at all?"

Gerry had a very apologetic look on his face. "Eight months…. credit for time served…two years probation and $25 million in restitution. That's all the DA could squeeze out of the judge after the police corruption angle was laid in there by Yevgrev's lawyers."

Muldoon's mouth was agape and his mind was frozen back in time. "That's it?"

Gerry nodded and added "He's out, Muldoon. He's out and I'm pretty sure he knows where you are…..and God knows, there was no love lost between you two."

"I've been gone for two years. How would he know where I live now?"

Gerry rubbed his hands together in a wringing motion before he spoke.

"The dirty cop was Peter Branderford, Muldoon. Your old partner."

Chapter Eighteen

Muldoon hadn't felt a blow to his chest like this since his father was murdered. Peter Branderford? How could that be?

"He was dirty by the time Yegrev got to him" stated Gerry "after you and he split and you went off to the Fraud Unit, he started buying and selling crack through *and* for his snitches.... one of the snitches turned him on to Yevgrev's supplier and then Peter went into the drug business big time."

"I don't get it" snapped Muldoon "what has this got to do with me?"

"Yevgrev found out that you and Peter used to be partners. He paid Peter a whole lot of money for information on you including your email account at the Fraud Unit. He knew just about every move you were making and when you used information drops, Peter was often the pick-up man."

"I can't believe this....why??......why Peter?"

"Apparently he had some ax to grind against you....something about you strutting around like you were the perfect cop and he was the bumbler."

"I never did that!!" Muldoon shouted "Never!"

"I never saw you do that....nobody did...but in Peter's mind he was never going to measure up and he decided in his head that *you* were the reason for it."

"This is crazy, Gerry…..none of this makes any sense to me. I mean, he's the Chief of Police now……how does a dirty cop get that job?"

"It gets worse, Muldoon…believe me."

Muldoon rubbed his forehead back and forth "This is like a nightmare….Yevgrev and Peter…..Jesus….I mean….why isn't Peter in jail if they found out he was dirty?"

"Peter knew….and Yevgrev knew that one of his shell companies was set up specifically to do business…..state government business…..building contracts and the like…..with the Governor's brother's big construction company…..all under the nose and approval of the Governor. Yevgrev had the Governor on tape and Peter had the tapes. Peter promised to release the tapes to the media unless all charges against him were dropped and his name was not mentioned."

"This goes up to the state capital??"

"Yep" said Gerry matter-of-factly "probably not quite enough to have the Governor tossed out but certainly enough for the "unfriendly" state legislators to give him a *very* bad time over every one of his proposals."

"And" Gerry continued "Peter didn't just demand that the charges be dropped……he wanted to stay on the force for the next three years so he could collect his pension."

"The tapes were that bad??"

"Bad enough. But Bill Channing, our own Chief of Police told the Governor, who he hates anyway, that there was no way he was going to have a dirty cop like Branderford on his force and if the Governor tried to shove that deal down his throat he'd go the media himself."

"This is like some bad Greek tragedy" said Muldoon "how did they get rid of Peter?"

"The Governor struck a deal with an old political pal of his by the name of Nick Spalata, Peter's predecessor. He was the Chief of Police up where you are until Peter brought his dirty little circus to town. Spalata had been the Chief up there for years and only had a year to go before he could retire with full benefits."

"I know who he is…..he lives across the lake from me."

"By all accounts he was a good guy but he owed the Governor some political favor from way back and the Governor convinced him to take "early retirement" with all his benefits so he could "appoint" Peter to replace him. That way Channing gets him out of his hair, the Governor gets to keep his job, Spalata gets to keep his benefits and Branderford gets to stay a cop for another three years until he retires."

"Awful…..just awful" replied Muldoon

"Sure is…..it's one big tar pit of bullshit, corruption and politics."

"And where is Yevgrev in all this?"

"From all accounts, he's keeping a low profile……but we both know that doesn't mean he's keeping his nose clean."

"Are he and Peter still in cahoots?"

"Can't say for certain……there's no real proof…..but did you ever know any leopards to change their spots?"

Muldoon just stared out the window – watching the big city move soundlessly to and fro 53 floors below. He wanted peace and quiet……he did not want to be part of Peter's dirty little circus.

"I'm sorry to have to be the bearer of such bad news, Muldoon…. but I felt like you had to know this. And I didn't want to tell you over the phone."

"Nothing I can do about it…..you think Peter's going to get all squirrely about me living up there on the lake?"

"He might……I've always thought he was a brick shy of a full load anyway…even way back when you two were partners…..there was just something not full square about him…..I was glad when you got on the Fraud Unit and could get rid of him….now there's all this going on."

Muldoon stood up and stretched his long arms above his head. He looked at Gerry for a minute and said "I'll tell you what I think…..I don't think Peter's going to do anything. He's held that job for what?…..almost three years now?"

Gerry nodded. "It'll be three years before the first snow falls."

"Then he gets to retire with all his benefits and pensions?"

"The full whack….that was the deal he made with the Governor." answered Gerry

"He's not going to rock that boat….no way….he wants the retirement money too badly."

"Well just in case…..we will, and by that I mean the Revona Group, will send up some security to keep an eye on him…..make sure he steers clear of you."

"Nice offer, Gerry. Thanks a lot……but I won't need it. I can handle Peter. I've *always* been able to handle Peter."

"It's no problem, buddy……just say the word and it's done…..you know, for old time's sake."

Muldoon shook his head again. "I'll be fine, Ger. Just fine."

Gerry rose to walk Muldoon back out to the lobby.

"You don't have any more bad news for me do you?" he asked with a grin.

"None that I can think of….but you'll be the first to know! Let me show you my office before you go."

They walked around the corner to the nice-sized and beautifully appointed office where Louise Rainer was seated…..and directly through to the huge and very impressive office that Gerry proudly stated was "my home away from home."

"Don't I know it!!" said the smartly dressed, attractive brunette seated on the couch.

It was Peter Brandeford's wife, Jennifer.

Chapter Nineteen

Muldoon was stunned. Jennifer looked neither embarrassed nor felt awkward. Gerry looked like he had just been "pipped at the post" by his girlfriend's presence. Muldoon waited for somebody to say something.

"Um.....I think you two know each other?" stammered Gerry

"Of course we do!" exclaimed Jennifer as she rose from the couch "What a surprise, Muldoon. How are you....what's it been....eight or nine years??"

"Good to see you, Jen. Yeah......I have to say this is quite a surprise." It was turning out to be a day of surprises.

"Honey, I just dropped by quickly to give you your ticket to the fundraiser tonight. I'll be backstage organizing things so you'll have to make the grand entrance all on your own." she joked

Just then Louise Rainer announced from the outer office "Mr. Dowling, it's Miss Beasley on line two....do you want to take the call?" Gerry nodded.

"Muldoon...we'll stay in touch, right? Please let me know if I can help in any way" he said as he shook his old pal's hand. "I'll *definitely* stay in touch, Ger. Thanks for the tips." was Muldoon's reply.

"Hey, Muldoon" said Jennifer "let me buy you a cup of coffee. There's a great diner around the corner and if I remember correctly you love diners as much as you love good coffee. We can catch up."

"Sure, Jen….that'd be nice. I still have a little time before I have to head for the heliport."

When they stepped into the empty elevator, Jennifer did not hesitate to break the silence. "It's not what you think, Muldoon. Gerry and I have been seriously dating for only a little more than four months."

"I'm trying not to think anything, Jen."

"I'd like to explain anyway."

"Are you sure I'm not going to need something stronger than a cup of coffee?" he said with his typical charming smile

"Well, it's a bit early for me and I have this big function tonight – but if you feel the need…"

They wound up at the Irish pub across the street from the diner. Muldoon needed fortification and a pint of Guinness seemed like a better deal than a cup of Greek coffee.

Muldoon did a fast track catch-up for Jennifer on his two-year globetrotting and she responded with updates on her two teenagers….neither of whom Muldoon had seen since they were six and four years old respectively.

"You wouldn't recognize them, Muldoon. Tim's a freshman in high school and has already earned his first athletic letter for swimming. And Chuck has turned into a computer wizard. He wants to study computer science when he gets to college."

"They sound like pretty good kids, Jen. You and Peter must be very proud."

"Well….I sure am and I tell them that all the time. Peter on the other hand never had anything good to say to them. I don't know what Gerry told you…"

"Everything" replied Muldoon

"They are better off without him….he was always too negative and they both had a rough time of things when Peter was trying to wiggle out of that grip that the Feds *and* that Russian had on him. It was a crazy, awful period. It took nearly every penny I had to get full custody of the boys. He got off scott-free from that deal he made with the Governor."

"Yeah….Ger told me."

"When I told him that I wanted out, he refused to believe me! He said I was just being unreasonable. He wanted us to go to marriage counseling!! Can you believe that? I told him that he was delusional and should go see a shrink on his own…..I was through with him."

"When was this?"

"The divorce and custody proceedings were finalized two years ago. I haven't seen him since then and am glad to be rid of him. When he got that new job, he still thought I was going to cave and move up there with him. He figured if the Governor gave him a "free pass" that I would, too. No way I was up for that. He was a rotten husband and father…….and a rotten cop too. About a year before he even cut his deal with the Governor, I told him that I was going to divorce him and take the kids."

Muldoon was beginning to feel that chill of a bad situation run through his veins. Jennifer's statement did not comport with what Ken mentioned about flying Peter down to the big city two or three times a month to "see his wife and kids."

"Nothing…..no contact at all?" he asked with an unusual worried tone.

"Nothing" repeated Jennifer "and he didn't believe it was happening right up until the end, either. A week before the divorce was final he said he had the perfect solution to bring me and the kids closer to him. And you know what he does? That lunatic comes home two hours later with a dog!!! Like there was going to be some immediate "Lassie effect" on our broken home and marriage!!"

Muldoon laughed at the idiocy of Peter's decision. It was vintage Peter Branderford.

"And not just any dog, mind you" chuckled Jen "you know what he brought home?"

Muldoon shook his head.

"A wolfhound!!!! An Irish wolfhound!! Do you know how big those dogs get to be....how much they eat!!?? He had the thing on a short leather leash and kept jerking the poor animal all over the apartment telling it to "Heel....heel". The poor little dog didn't know which end was up."

Muldoon felt his chest seriously tightening. He began to feel nauseous.

"I mean.....keeping an Irish wolfhound in an apartment here in the big city?!....that just shows you how out of touch with reality Peter was. I told him to get out and take the dog with him."

Muldoon found it difficult to speak. "What did he do?" he said through a clenched jaw.

"I'm not sure. That was the last time I saw him. He didn't even show up at the final court session.....sent his lawyer and that was it. I think he must have taken that dog with him up to his new place. He got a small house up in that small town where he had just been "appointed" the new police chief. If he did, I pity that poor animal......Peter treated his sons like dirt and they were his own flesh and blood. Can you imagine what he'd do to a dog?"

Muldoon excused himself for a moment and headed to the Men's Room where he vomited violently.

When he returned to the bar he was too pale for Jennifer not to notice. "Are you OK, Muldoon?"

He nodded. "Might just be a little early for a pint of Guinness.... even for me." he answered trying to deflect the situation.

"Listen, Jen.....I have a helicopter pilot waiting to take me back to Frettyman Lake."

"Frettyman??.....that's near where Peter is."

"Yeah" admitted Muldoon "he came out to the lake to see me last week."

"Muldoon, please don't tell him that you've seen me....I can't..."

Muldoon interrupted her. "This meeting...this conversation never happened, Jen. Trust me. I won't say a word."

She thanked him and reached for the bar bill. Muldoon tried to cut her off but she insisted. "For old time's sake" she winked "and to make up for all those wicked dates I set you up on!!"

The color was beginning to return to Muldoon face at the recollection of them. "Some weren't so bad, Jen.....believe me."

"Yeah .....I heard" she smiled "Girls talk, buddy!"

He walked her out to the street and gave her a nice hug before she stepped into a taxi. "We'll meet again, Muldoon. Maybe you and me and Ger can have a night out....no blind dates, I promise!"

"Anytime."

As her taxi pulled away, Muldoon immediately reached into his trousers' pocket to get his cell phone. He phoned Patrick to make certain that everything was OK with Mugsy.

"He's great, Mr. Frickey...no problems. What a great dog. Personality for days!!"

Muldoon explained that he'd probably be home in just a little over an hour. "Keep a watchful eye over Mugsy 'til I get there... OK.?"

"Sure will....Doc Carlin is here, too. Do you want to speak to him?"

Muldoon said yes and asked Doc to stay with Patrick until he got home.

"Be happy to" said Doc "everything OK?"

"Yep" said Muldoon "but if you don't mind, stay with Patrick and I'll be back up at the lake in an hour or so."

He hopped into a taxi and told the driver to take him to the heliport.

"Step on it" he instructed the driver. And he *meant* it.

Chapter Twenty

Ken watched from the manager's office as Muldoon got out of the taxi and reached in the passenger's window to give the driver his fare and a nice tip. "Good driving. You blew through that rush hour traffic in no time. Thanks."

Ken waved him into the office. "Have a seat here while I fire the bird up." He introduced him to Kevin, the heliport manager. "Don't let that dejected look on Kevin's face fool you….he's normally a very cheery guy, but I have been beating him at gin rummy for the past four and a half hours!! He's probably very glad to see you…..it means that I have to leave!" Kevin simply responded by saying that the deck must have been stacked.

They were in the air in no time. Muldoon was not so much sullen as he was pre-occupied with the information overload he received from both Gerry and Jennifer.

"How was your meeting?" asked Ken trying to make mindless conversation.

It broke Muldoon out of his reflective stupor and he responded by saying rather mindlessly "Ah…..it was OK….pretty good meeting as meetings come and go….I never liked meetings much anyway."

"Personally, I never could stand them….they always went on too long…I think most of them are just a huge waste of time, myself." said Ken

"Yeah….." agreed Muldoon "a lot of them are…..this one wasn't, but…yeah …a lot of meetings are useless. This one, though, was worth going to. But, I am glad to be heading home. This flight sure beats the mind-numbing drive back."

"Like I said, I do it so much I could handle it with my eyes closed – if it wasn't deadly dangerous!! I'm doing it again next week with Chief Branderford – up and back the same day – just like always."

Muldoon surveyed the horizon briefly before he commented. "Listen, Ken….you know I've been doing some investigative work on the Skudnick case, right?" Ken nodded. "I'd appreciate it if you didn't mention to the Chief that you flew me down to the big city or that you and I discussed the case. I don't want him to get the idea that I'm interfering."

"You're a licensed private investigator….why would he think you are interfering?"

"Being a former cop myself, I know how cops think…..it just would be better not to say anything, if you don't mind."

"No problem" said Ken "he never says much of anything anyway…..he won't sit up front….ever….so it's hard to make con-versation. He's always plopped in the back there in the plush seats…..spends the whole time mostly sending texts on his cell phone. I always ask him how the wife and kids are and all he ever says is "Good…..I miss them" or "my wife's coming up here soon, but she'll drive 'cause she doesn't like to fly" and that about the extent of conversation with him."

"He never stays overnight?" asked Muldoon knowing full well that if he did, it was definitely not with Jennifer.

"Nope….not as long as I've been flying him. Never travels in uniform, either. He says the trips are not official police busi-ness……strictly family oriented. He just carries a small sport bag…same one every time…must be one from when he was on the force in the big city 'cause it has the logo on it…and he's always dressed very casually. He's an odd duck, that guy."

"Odd" was not the word for Peter Branderford thought Muldoon. But he did not want to think about him anymore right now and changed the subject.

"I sure could use a cold one!" he said to Ken "too bad you can't set this baby right on the roof of The Belly Up!"

"I've often suggested that to Pietro, believe me" laughed Ken "after I've had a few too many! But 'My suitisgone' is already half the size of that shanty old place!! The noise from me trying to set it down there would scare half the old drunks right out into the street!!"

"Don't want to do that!" said Muldoon

"Naw….those old guys really love that place….don't want to scare them out. Hell….I love that place!"

"Yeah….I'm beginning to as well" replied Muldoon with Patticake on his mind.

"It's usually a pretty nice crowd in there…..except for one."

"Who's that?" asked Muldoon with no real interest in what the answer would be.

"Lutursky……that old bastard Larry Lutursky you must have seen him….lurks at the dark end of the bar."

Muldoon knew right off who Ken meant. "Yeah….now that you mention it, I have seen him a few times. Speaking of odd ducks….he sure strikes me as one."

"Damn straight. He's all that and more. He gives me the shivers….always has."

Muldoon didn't want to focus on Larry Lutursky or Peter Branderford for that matter. He wanted to get home to Mugsy.

He had a pretty good idea of how he was going to deal with Peter if he came snooping around and Larry was The Belly Up's problem.

Or so he thought.

Chapter Twenty-One

Muldoon gave a big wave and shouted to Ken "See you at The Belly Up!" as he stepped on the gas and drove a fast eight miles back to his cabin on the lake. Mugsy heard him pull up and trotted from around the back yard where Doc and Patrick were watching over him.

He crouched down to beckon him near "C'mere you old ruffian you….get over here for a hug!" Mugsy trotted straight into his arms and Muldoon stroked the back of his neck. "You're a good old dog, Mugsy….and you're safe with me. You'll always be safe with me."

The two of them rounded the cabin to the back deck. "Hello fellas" he said to Doc and Patrick "everything good on Frettyman Lake?" Doc smiled and Patrick said he'd been admiring Muldoon's Indian canoe. "Well, if you like to fish, I'll take you out one of these days."

"You look tired, Muldoon" said Doc.

"A bit" he acknowledged "being in the big city can be tiring…..I guess I'm not used to it anymore. How do you think Mugsy looks, Doc?"

"Astonishingly well, if I do say so myself. He's not even the same dog that was housed in a cage in the pound. He's bounced back faster than any dog I've seen in a long time. Look how nicely certain parts of his coat are starting to shine again."

"Yeah..." interjected Patrick "we gave him a bath earlier this afternoon!"

"He didn't mind?" questioned Muldoon

"Not a bit....I kind of held him still and Doc did the shampooing."

"I was pleased that he held with basic strangers for so long and even more pleased that he didn't really flinch when I rubbed over the side where his ribs were cracked."

Muldoon got a mental image of Peter Branderford beating his beloved Mugsy and had to shake clear of it before he started seeing red.

"Doc, let me ask you something" he said as he gently stroked Mugsy head "you've been attending to dogs at the pound for how long now?"

"Oh, Lord...must be twenty years at least....seems like forever!" replied Doc

"Before 'ol Mugsy was stretchered in nearly dead, when was the last Irish Wolfhound you attended to at the pound?"

"None.....Mugsy was the first." was Doc's quick reply

"You absolutely certain of that?"

"Definitely.....Mugsy was the first and only. Kitty told me you came in asking for an Irish Wolfhound.....your timing was perfect!"

"Just lucky I guess." said Muldoon

"I think Mugsy's the lucky one, if you ask me" added Patrick "you've got a great home for him here."

Muldoon said it was high time he started driving Patrick home. But first he gave him a crisp $100 bill.

"That's a little more than we agreed upon, Mr. Frickey. You only owe me $80."

"A man who does a good job is entitled to a little extra – my old man taught me that!"

Patrick put the C note in his jeans and said "Well, then I will thank BOTH Mr. Frickeys!"

"Muldoon, there's no reason for both of us to drive back into town. I'll take Patrick home. You sit and relax....put your feet up...take a load off. You've had a long day. "

"Thanks, Doc. I could use a little downtime. Maybe I'll take Mugsy inside, light a fire, make a big batch of popcorn and put on an old movie."

"Sounds like a good plan to me." said Doc

"You like old movies, Mr. Frickey?" asked Patrick. Muldoon nodded "Love 'em."

"What are you going to watch?"

"I think I'll get into 'Stalag 17' tonight. I'm in the mood for it."

"I know that one!" exclaimed Patrick "I was in our high school production of it when I was a freshman."

"Is that the one with William Holden and the prisoners?" wondered Doc

"That's the one....well, that's the movie version.....I don't know who was in the original play.....but they all think that Sefton, this guy played by William Holden, is the stooge who's getting everybody killed but it's really this other guy...this guy who's a spy for the Nazis." explained Patrick

"That's the one, alright" said Muldoon "just goes to show you that you have to be careful who you put the finger on! You want to make sure you shoot the right guy!"

"Good advice if you're a prisoner of war!!" laughed Doc

"Good advice for anywhere" Muldoon said to both of them as he walked them around to the front cabin.

"Oh...Mr. Frickey...before I forget....Lou called me....said that he wanted to talk to you."

"Lou?"

"Yeah....you remember my friend Lou, the plumber? Well....
he's *studying* to be a plumber.....he's got the fruit and veg stand next
to the parking lot....you remember?"

"Oh, yeah...sure....of course.....now I remember...I was just
a little pre-occupied. Doc, you're sure about that now....about
Mugsy being the only Irish Wolfhound?"

"No question about it...he was the one and only....that's what
we should call him – The One and Only Mugsy!"

"That's what he looks like to me -- the one and only!" stated
Patrick "but anyway, Mr. Frickey....Lou really wants you to call
him...here's his number."

"Did he say it was urgent......'cause I'm really in the mood for
this movie now!"

"No, he didn't say it was urgent......but he did say it was
important, though."

"OK...I'll give him a ring.....after the movie! Thanks for
your help today, fellas."

"Anytime, Mr. Frickey....you need help with Mugsy -- you
call me anytime."

Doc drove down the road and Muldoon gave Mugsy a little
tap on the side.

"C'mon boy....inside we go.....we'll watch this old movie and
make sure we still remember how to finger the right guy."

Chapter Twenty-Two

Muldoon's fitful night of sleep did not sit well with him in the morning. He'd always been a great sleeper and all he did last night was toss and turn. He couldn't get out of his head what Gerry Dowling and Jennifer Branderford told him about Peter. Even while he was watching "Stalag 17", his mind kept drifting and he realized in the morning that he was letting events overwhelm him. He always prided himself on his ability to stay on top of all situations. It was a trait he picked up from his father. But this time, he just could not get in front of this situation. Most importantly, the peace and quiet he so treasured looked like it might be interfered with and that, above all, displeased Muldoon.

He did everything he thought he could do to take his mind off the "Peter problem". He made breakfast, spent time with Mugsy out in the back of the cabin, cleaned out the fireplace, cleaned up the kitchen, took out the garbage and gathered a bunch of shirts to be dry cleaned. None of these distractions really worked, but the cabin was neat and clean! Muldoon thought that was alright because he liked things orderly.

Then he remembered that he was supposed to phone Lou, the plumber.

When he got a hold of him, Lou asked if they could meet at The Belly Up at noon.

"Kind of early for a drink, isn't it, Lou?" was Muldoon's response

"Have a club soda.....I just need someplace nearby to meet you."

The meet was set for High Noon.

On his way in town. Muldoon saw Peter moving quickly coming out of the diner while he was stuck at the traffic light. He honked his horn and waved. "No reason to let him think I want to be unfriendly" thought Muldoon "no reason to let him raise an eyebrow about me or anything I am doing."

Peter started to run quickly across the street to his parked squad car. Muldoon waved out the side window "Where's the fire, Chief? You look like you're in a big hurry."

Peter returned the wave in a half-hearted fashion and jumped into his car. He turned the flashing siren on atop his car roof and let it wail. Then he stepped on the gas and headed in the opposite direction.

"I wonder what all *that* was about?" said Muldoon to no one. He parked his car in the lot and walked straight for The Belly Up.

The first thing he saw was Patti-cake facing the cash register setting up the bar money for the day. He thought she looked as good from the back as she did from the front. There was no sign of Lou but Muldoon wasn't the first one in the bar. Larry Lutursky was already seated in his perch at the far end.

"You are distractingly attractive, you know that?" said Muldoon

Patti-cake made a half turn and winked at him. "And you are handsome but unreliable. Anybody ever tell you that?" Muldoon just stared and smiled. "I never know when you are coming in. Most of my customers have a regular pattern they keep."

"Sorry about that, Patti-cake – but I'm still a full-time hard working man. I have business to attend to. Lots of your custom-ers have left the rat race" Then he leaned over and whispered to her "Like whats-his-name down there at the end of the bar."

"I'm not sure if he *ever* had a regular job --- besides drink-ing!" she said adjusting her blouse. "What are you having today, Muldoon?"

No more waiting. Muldoon went flat out. "Dinner with you......my house...tonight....after you get off work....you have no idea how well I can cook...I'll pick you up and drive you home after coffee and dessert."

Patti-cake hesitated for a moment.

"C'mon Patti-cake.....get off that 'maybe' square you're stand-ing in.....move to the 'yes' square......I've had a rough couple days... and I need to be in some female company that doesn't include looking at Mr. Ugly down there in my peripheral vision."

"Well.....I don't drink coffee – so get some tea.....and just so you know.....I'm not going to be dessert!"

"Whatever you want." said Muldoon "I'll be back to pick you up at seven o'clock."

"You leaving already? You haven't even had anything to drink."

Lou walked in the front door and heard the last part of Patti-cake's sentence.

"He'll probably be wanting a club soda!"

"Hi Lou!!" said Patti-cake "Gosh.....to what do I owe this honor? You're hardly ever here in the daytime. I only see you when I walk over to your fruit and veg stand!"

"It's a special occasion. I have business here with Mr. Frickey."

Lou and Muldoon sat at the table next to the front window after taking a bottle of Budweiser and a club soda set down by Patti-cake.

"So…what's on your mind, Lou?"

Lou explained that he had been keeping his eyes and ears to the ground for any strange goings on in The Belly Up at nights – especially Saturday or any unusual comings and goings on the street -- or at least whatever he could spot from his fruit and veg stand.

"I didn't see anything too unusual. But the other day, I had an apprentice assignment to bleed some radiators down by the old railroad tracks. There's twelve unit blocks of public housing down there ---- sort of like 'projects'….they're pretty run down for only being forty years old. But it's all low-income housing. There's some Asians who live there but mostly its Latinos. So I asked if I could bring my pal, Tony, with me who is also an apprentice plumber and he speaks fluent Spanish."

"And….?"

"Well, we have to knock on all the doors and announce who we are and what we are going to do. Not everybody let's you in….. the trust factor is not too high down there for white strangers."

"Go on…"

"Well" continued Lou "we're in one apartment and the woman….no… it was two women….both dressed in black and black veils on their heads. There were a couple of teenagers in there too….maybe eighteen or nineteen years old. I couldn't understand what they were talking about, but they were obviously grieving over something."

"How long were you in the apartment?" asked Muldoon.

"Not more than twenty minutes or so….half an hour tops. But here's the kicker….after we left, Tony takes me into the stair landing and says that he thinks we just were in the apartment of the family of that Esperanza girl who died with the Skutnick kid."

"Are you sure?"

"Well, Tony was pretty sure. He understood what they were saying and he said there was a lot of angry talk about finding out who killed the girl.....I mean they *really* wanted to find out who gave her the drugs. Tony said one of the women said she was going to wear black until the day they found out who it was who killed her pretty little girl."

"So it *was* Esperanza who brought the drugs to Paul's house that night....not the other way around."

"Apparently so. Tony said one of the teenagers was talking about taking out the 'white bastard' who lived down the hall..... Apartment 35 they kept saying."

"Did they know for sure that this guy in Apartment 35 gave Esperanza the ecstasy?"

"Tony couldn't hear everything they were saying because the two teenagers were in the kitchen.....but he said that they kept calling him the 'white bastard supplier'.....the way they were talking to one of the women wearing the veils, Tony heard that it was one of Esperanza's girlfriends that told one of the teenagers there in the kitchen on the day she was buried that Esperanza told her that she was bringing two ecstasy pills with her over to Paul's house that night to liven things up."

"And they were talking about killing him.....this guy down the hall??!!"

"It sure sounded like that to Tony. So we went down to the lobby and checked to see if there was a name on the mailbox or buzzer."

"What did you find?.....anything?"

"Sure did.....the name next to Apartment 35 on the buzzer is 'W. Skudnick'.

Muldoon was stunned into silence and all he could do for a moment was stare at Lou. His findings finally registered with Muldoon and he said "You mean to tell me that Wally Skutnick lives in the same building as the family of the girl who died along with his son from bad drugs?"

"Not just the same building, Muldoon....the same floor!!"

"Did you knock on his door....was he home?"

"I knocked alright. His apartment has a radiator in it that I'm supposed to bleed but he wasn't home. I left an official notice on his door, like I'm supposed to do."

Muldoon was beginning to envision a worst case scenario where Wally Skudnick could have supplied the ecstasy pill that killed his own son. He tried not to make a judgment or arrive at a conclusion without a full set of facts but there was a major set of coincidental information starting to gel in his mind.

He had to think clearly if he was going to be able to analyze the facts correctly and what was clear was that he needed more facts.

"Lou" he said "can you come with me now.....take me over to Skudnick's place?"

"Sure....be happy to. I'm not actually required to go back there for a second try until Wednesday but I can show you exactly where it is."

"Great....let's get a move on because I have a funny feeling about this guy. I want to talk to him. Does it take long to get over there?"

Nope...we can head out on the road past the diner....we'll go the back way....should take about ten or fifteen minutes."

They both got up from the table and Muldoon brought his empty glass and Lou's empty beer bottle back to the bar. "I'll see you at 7:00 pm" he whispered to Patti-cake.

"You two leaving already?"

"Got some business to attend to."

"Yeah!" added Lou excitedly "me and Mr. Frickey have some *business* to attend to!!"

They left – leaving Patti- cake alone with Larry Lutursky.

Chapter Twenty-Three

By the time Lou directed Muldoon through the maze of back roads and they arrived in the front of the building where Wally Skudnick lived, they both could tell that there was something seriously amiss. There was an ambulance with its siren off but the red light still flashing. Next to the ambulance was Peter Branderford's squad car. No flashing light on its roof but the presence of both those vehicles spelled some trouble on the rise. Muldoon knew now where Peter was flying off to when he saw him running out of the diner earlier. He noticed that the area had not yet been cordoned off with familiar-looking yellow "crime scene" tape.

"This looks bad to me, Muldoon" said a worried Lou.

"Let's go have a look" replied Muldoon "it might not be as bad as you think. I've seen worse scenes than this in the big city."

"This isn't the big city. This is a small town and for a small town like this one.....this looks bad."

Muldoon motioned for Lou to follow him. "Are you sure?" asked Lou. Just as they were approaching the front door of the building, out walked Peter Branderford.

"Hold it right there." he said in his most growly, officious Chief of Police tone of voice. "You can't come in here."

Muldoon motioned for Lou to step back a little but he, himself, continued towards Peter.

"What are you doing here, Muldoon?" demanded Peter

"I came to see somebody who lives in this building" he replied very calmly "any law against that?"

"Exactly who?" demanded Peter again "and what is _he_ doing with you?" he said pointing aggressively at Lou

Muldoon made the instantaneous decision that he was not going to get into an argument with Peter, whose temper was well known to him. So, again he replied very calmly. "Don't you worry about him…..he's with me. Is this a crime scene, Peter?"

"No" answered Peter abruptly.

Before Muldoon could ask his next question, two ambulance attendants rolled a stretcher out the front door. On top of the stretcher was a black body bag…all zipped up.

Muldoon looked at Peter and then at the body bag….then back again at Peter.

"Who's that?"

"_That_" said Peter pointing with disgust at the body bag "is Wanda Skudnick – shot three times right through the chest."

Muldoon tried not to react too severely or obviously. "And you are telling me that this is not a crime scene?"

"Self-defense is not a crime. Surely you remember that from your Academy training." scoffed Peter

"Who in the world would have to defend themselves against Wanda Skudnick?"

"Her ex-husband" declared Peter

Lou was listening and nearly exploded at what he overheard. "Are you saying that that scumbag Wally Skudnick shot his ex-wife to death!!!"

Muldoon turned quickly and motioned for Lou to settle down.

"What business is it of yours anyway……who are you to be asking the Chief of Police anything?" Peter yelled

"OK....OK....Pete....never mind it....I told you he was with me. Besides, *is* that what really happened, if you don't mind my asking?"

"What has this got to do with you anyway, Muldoon?"

"I was doing some investigative work for Wanda."

"What kind of investigative work......if you don't mind *my* asking." snapped Peter

"*Private* investigative work......that's what kind."

"Well now, it sure does look like your *private* investigative work for Wanda Skudnick it's over, isn't it?.......your client is dead."

Muldoon was beginning to see red. When he looked at Peter now all he could see was a dirty cop.....a dirty cop and a liar.....all he could hear was that nagging smugness that he had always hated in Peter's voice.

"What are you going to do with the body?"

"Not that it's any business of yours, but it's going to the morgue. She doesn't have any living relatives being that her drug-addicted son is already dead...so it'll sit there and then eventually be dumped into a pauper's grave. A fitting end for a shitty mother."

"How do you know what kind of mother she was?" Muldoon blurted out

"Look what happened to her kid....if she was doing her job as a mother right, the kid would never have wound up on drugs."

Lou became infuriated at that last statement "Listen, you useless shit...my friend Paul was NOT on drugs!!!"

Peter moved right to where Lou was standing and shoved him in the shoulder "You feel like goin' to jail, plumber-boy?"

Muldoon darted quickly to place himself between Peter and Lou before Lou planted his fist directly onto Peter's nose. "Lou!!" he shouted "stand back!"

He placed himself smack dab in front of Peter – face to face – with his feet firmly planted on the ground. It was a position he'd had to put himself in countless times when Peter was ready to beat one of their street snitches to a pulp.

"Let it go, Pete…..you don't want any trouble from me, believe me. I told you Lou was with me….so back off."

"You should be more careful about the company you keep, Muldoon. You could get a bad reputation. It's a small town."

"I can take care of myself……always could. I don't need to remind *you* of that." Muldoon barked.

"And" he continued "I don't want any advice from you about the kind of company I should keep."

He walked away from the crime-scene-that-was-not-a-crime-scene and told Lou to follow him. He had just lost his cool in front of his ex-partner, the dirty cop.

He had just said too much……one sentence too much and he knew it.

Chapter Twenty-Four

"Direct me back to The Belly Up, Lou......on the back roads....same way we got out here."

Lou complied with a series of directions. "Turn right here.... turn left here....straight ahead....left again at the bottom of the hill"....on and on until Muldoon recognized the road leading up to the diner from the back side. When Muldoon pulled into the parking lot next to the German Meat Market there had not been more than a dozen words exchanged between the two. Muldoon didn't feel like talking and Lou did not know what to say. After Muldoon turned the ignition off Lou finally spoke.

"You really stood up to him back there. You stood up for me against him. I want to thank you for that.....in two and a half years I have never seen anybody back Branderford down like that. But, I also got the strange feeling that you and he know each other.... like you two didn't just meet for the first time here."

Muldoon knew the time had come to 'fess up. He blew his cool and his cover in front of a pretty intelligent twenty-one year old plumber-to-be and he knew he had to tell him the truth. He owed him that much.

"You're right" he said "Very observant. I know Peter from a long time ago."

"From where?" Lou persisted

"What I tell you now you keep under your hat, you hear me? Not a word to anybody...you got that?"

Lou nodded silently as his body tensed up.

"Peter Branderford was assigned to be my partner on the force in the big city twelve years ago. We were partners for three years and it ended nine years ago. I hardly ever ran into him after I joined the Fraud Unit. I was a fraud investigator for seven years and then retired from the force....travelled around the world for two years and then moved here. I had no idea Peter was the Chief of Police up here until he showed up at my cabin."

"OK.....I get that" said Lou "seeing him again in our small town was just a matter of coincidence. But, that doesn't explain why you practically threatened him back there...because that's sure what it sounded like to me."

Muldoon knew that Lou needed one more piece of information or he'd wind up making assumptions and drawing the wrong conclusions.

"He's a dirty cop, Lou. He knows he's a dirty cop and I know he's a dirty cop....now you know it."

"But, I don't see how..."

Muldoon cut him short. "That's all the information you are getting right now. It's all you need to know. Don't even *pretend* to anybody that you know anything about him. He's a dangerous man and you don't know how to deal with that kind of danger. Do you understand me? Do you and I have a complete understanding on this?"

Lou whispered "Yes" as though he thought Chief Branderford might be listening.

"Good" said Muldoon bluntly "now come with me into The Belly Up.....I need you to help me plan Wanda Skudnick's funeral mass and burial."

"How are going to get anybody to release her body to you....

you're not a relative."

"Lou...if there is anything you should know about me at all it's that when I decide I am going to do something.....I do it. Plain and simple. No questions asked. I simply don't allow anyone to get in my way."

When they got to the curb waiting for the traffic light to change, Lou looked Muldoon straight in the eye and said "You're going to get Branderford aren't you?'

The light changed and Muldoon started to cross the street and said without looking at Lou "Focus on the task at hand, my friend. Right now we are going to see to it that Wanda Skudnick gets a proper and respectful burial."

News travels fast in a small town.

When Lou and Muldoon walked in, The Belly Up was already crowded with customers who were shocked and stunned at the news travelling around that Wally Skudnick murdered his wife. Information was being re-wound, ground up, reflected against a shoddy set of facts and spread like it was the gospel truth. Truth was...nobody knew what they were talking about but the shots and the beers compelled them to talk anyway. The Belly Up had become The Babble Up. Barry the Gambler was having a field day correcting what he perceived to be other people's misinformation and miscommunications that, in fact, began with his big announcement an hour ago that there had been a murder..... a "revenge murder" over in the projects "where the poor people live." Once he got started he was hard to stop.

Every seat at the bar was taken and there were a couple dozen more customers milling around – all of them in one way or another knew Wanda or knew about Wally and his bad reputation. Some of them had kids who went to school with Paul. They all knew that Paul had recently died and could not believe that his mother was following him to her grave so soon. The impact of a double tragedy is augmented when there is less of a population to spread it thinly through. And the news of this tragedy was obviously having a dramatic impact on this small town's population. The devastating rumors were swilling everywhere. What to believe and what not to believe was no longer the order of the day. Everybody thought they were right and they thought everybody else was wrong. There were recriminations and remonstrations in between the teardrops and sniffles. It was hard to tell who needed comfort. But it was easy to see that nearly everyone was in pain.

All except one, that is. All the tide of high emotions ran lost and wandering right through Larry Lutursky. He was unmoved and unconcerned. He wanted more shots of Jack Daniels and kept tapping his empty shot glass on the bar to attract Patti-cake's attention until she finally snapped at him.

"Stop tapping that shot glass!!!" she screamed

"Then give me what I want!" he yelled back.

That was all Ken, who was seated at the front of the bar next to Doc Carlin, needed to hear. He jumped up from his seat and headed towards Larry. "I'll give you what you want you son-of-a-bitch!!" He nearly knocked Doc out of his seat in the process.

Muldoon grabbed him by the arm and said "Easy, Ken....you can't go hitting a guy who's nearly eighty years old......it's a losing proposition for you."

The crowd and commotion drew Peitro up from the downstairs where he had been working on the books. He took one look at Patti-cake, who was already distraught from the news of Wanda's death, and asked her what was going on.

"Get that old bastard out of here. I can't deal with him today."

Pietro immediately cleared Larry's empty shot glass and half empty bottle of beer away from him and simply said "Leave. The lady does not want you here."

"I ain't finished." he snarled

"You are now" said Pietro with a look in his eyes that *really* said "you just might be finished for good."

"I gotta take a leak." Larry stated

"Then take your leak and leave. And be quick about it."

Larry walked right into the Ladies Room before anyone could stop him and locked the door. In less time than it would have taken a healthy twenty-year old guy to pee, Larry was finished and opened the door. Ken was standing next to Pietro when he came out. "I told you before to stay out of the Ladies john. I don't want to see you use it again." said the angry helicopter pilot

"And I told you before it ain't none of your business. Get out of my way!" Larry was holding his cane in his hand and from the front of the bar it looked to Lou like the cane was broken.

"Leave him go, Ken" said Pietro "Go on Larry ...get out of here."

Like father...like son --- Pietro was doing the same thing his father used to do 60 years ago – throwing Larry Lutursky out of The Belly-Up.

While Larry made a big deal about it and shoved his way out the back door, Lou slipped out, unnoticed, through the front one.

He walked around the side of the bar to where he could see Larry walking out of the parking lot area that was directly outside the bar's back door. When he thought he was far enough away from the bar, Larry stopped.

What Lou watched him do raised the hairs on the back of his neck. Larry unscrewed the top portion of his cane – the hook – pounded the stick on the sidewalk a couple of times and then screwed the hook back in to place. He looked around to see if anyone saw him and continued on down the sidewalk.

He didn't see Lou. But Lou knew exactly what he saw and went straight back into The Belly-Up to tell Muldoon.

Chapter Twenty-Five

Muldoon guessed right that between Doc Carlin and Ken, they knew just about everybody in town. When he explained to them that he wanted to organize a proper funeral for Wanda, their immediate reaction was "what can we do to help?"

Doc said that he knew the coroner very well when Muldoon said that the first thing they had to do was get her body over to the local funeral director who, coincidentally, was married to Ken's cousin. "I need to have the body released to a non-family member, Doc. Do you think that will be a problem?"

"Shouldn't be" said Doc "if the coroner's report says that this was a case of self-defense, there won't be an inquest. I'll let him know what you're doing and there won't be any complications.'

"Same with my cousin's husband" added Ken "I'll give him the low-down and there won't be any questions asked."

"Thanks fellas. I'll feel better if Wanda is laid to rest with some dignity. And money is no object, Ken....so tell your cousin's husband to pick out a nice casket."

They were about to discuss who would contact the parish priest and arrange for the Mass when Kitty Selarus walked in. Her eyes were red from crying but she was composed enough to think that there might be a gathering at The Belly Up.

Doc got up from his bar stool and offered it to the brokenhearted Kitty. "I'm real sorry about all this, Kitty. I know Wanda was your best friend."

Kitty softly acknowledged Doc's sympathetic overture. She paused a moment before she spoke. "Self-defense?....is that the rumor I'm hearing?....that feckless punk of an ex-husband is claiming that he shot my friend Wanda in self defense?"

Muldoon explained that Branderford said there were no witnesses and Wally, indeed, claimed he shot Wanda in self-defense.

"And exactly what was Wanda armed with? asked Kitty.

"She didn't have to be armed, Kitty. It was only necessary that Wally felt like his life was being threatened." answered Muldoon

"That gutter-snipe spent years and years threatening Wanda. He spent years using her and Paul as punching bags and she never tried to shoot *him*. Now this!!...and he walks away?"

Muldoon nodded said again "There were no witnesses."

"I told her not to go over there....I told her that there'd be trouble." cried Kitty

"What do you mean?" asked Doc

"Wanda phoned me at the pound this morning. She said that she got some strange call saying that her ex-husband knew inside information about how her son died. She told me that this stranger's voice said Wally was getting ready to skip town and when he left he'd be taking the information with him so if she wanted to find out anything, she'd better get over there before it was too late. She was very, very upset at the thought that Wally might have had something to do with Paul's death. She was agitated, half-hysterical, half-crying and nearly out of her mind with grief."

"Who was this caller......a man or a woman?" asked Muldoon

"She said it was some man....didn't know who it was....she said it was obvious that he was trying to disguise his voice....but she had no idea who it was. She asked what I thought she should do."

"What did you tell her?" said Doc

"I told her to ignore it....forget about it....it was probably some crank call anyway. I told her that we both knew Wally lived in a bad section of town ....it wasn't safe for her to go there."

"Did she agree with you?"

"She wasn't making any sense......she kept saying she was so confused. So, I told her to get in her car and come over to the pound. ....we could try and make some sense of all this."

"Did she agree to that?" asked Muldoon

"Yes....she said she would get in her car and drive over as soon as she calmed down.......I think she might have calmed down but I think she got into her car and drove over to Wally's place to confront him instead of coming over to the pound."

Kitty stared into space and rubbed her temples... "And now she's dead.....this is just unbelievable.....my best friend is dead and there's nothing I can do."

"You can help us plan her funeral, Kitty" said Doc "Muldoon, here, is picking up the tab and we're going to give her a nice send-off."

Kitty wiped her eyes and grabbed Muldoon's forearm "You're a good man, Muldoon. I knew that the first time you walked into the dog pound."

Muldoon assigned Kitty the task of coordinating with the parish priest for the Mass and Ken agreed to get everything moving with the funeral director and the cemetery. Doc was in charge of getting the body released and volunteered to make sure that there'd be plenty of nice flowers at the funeral home.

"Oh. Kitty" said Muldoon "there's one more thing you can do.....can you ask Patrick to tell all his friends.....tell him to use that "Tweet" thing they all use....I think that there should be a big representation at the wake and Mass for their friend Paul's mother."

"I'll make sure of it" answered Kitty "there'll be a lot of folks there, don't worry. A lot of people liked Wanda."

"Good. I want this to be a nice service." he said "What sort of headstone is there now up at Paul's gravesite?"

"Just a flat marker in the ground. Wanda couldn't think of anything else at the time because she was so grieved. She mentioned that she might put up something more formal but ..."

"It's OK, Kitty. Don't worry about it." assured Muldoon "Ken ....when you talk to the guy at the cemetery make sure you have him arrange for a double headstone...room enough for both Paul and Wanda's names....and make sure he gets the birth and death dates correct....he can probably get them from the coroner."

"Consider it done" answered Ken

"It *is* a double plot isn't it, Kitty" asked Muldoon

She nodded. "It's the burial plot that she and Wally bought just after they got married."

"He's a cursed bastard" chimed Doc

"We can't worry about Wally right now....let's get Wanda the service she deserves and then we'll take care of the rest later." said Muldoon

"I'm going back to the pound now, Muldoon. I sure do appreciate everything you are doing here."

"Kitty...do you have a way to get into Wanda's house.....the funeral director will need a set of clothes to lay her out in." asked Muldoon

"I have a set of keys.....I'll go over later....after work and pick out something nice."

"Let me walk you back to the pound" said Doc "it's time for me to get home anyway."

They said their goodbyes and Muldoon assured them that if any of them needed anything to smooth the funeral arrangements along, all they had to do was call him – anytime day or night.

Lou was standing at the side of the bar waiting for Doc, Ken and Kitty to leave. After they walked out the door he approached Muldoon and said "I didn't want to interrupt your chat about funeral plans but I *have* to tell you something....and I didn't want anybody else to hear it."

He whispered to Muldoon exactly what he watched Larry Lutursky do after he stormed out the back door of The Belly Up.

"What??" exclaimed Muldoon

"That's what I said" repeated Lou "the top of his cane screws off...it's actually two separate parts....the stick and the hook. And it sure looked to me that Larry wanted to make sure that nobody saw him taking the hook off and screwing it back on tight while he was out there in the street.....he had a very paranoid look on his face."

"How did you notice this?" asked Muldoon

"Do you remember when he came out of the Ladies' Room and had shouting match with Ken about him using it? It was then. He was holding his hand over the part where the hook screws in.....like he wanted to cover it up or something. I thought it looked strange because when you hold a cane like that, you can't use it properly....you have to have your hand on the hook. But he was making such a bluster about getting out the back door I don't think anyone paid any attention to it....they were just glad to see the back of him."

"And out in the street he fixed it?"

"Yep. When he thought nobody was looking."

Muldoon tried to think of why Larry Lutursky would *not* want anybody to know that he had an adjustable cane. Sometimes people had them for style...different hooks for different occasions or looks....sometimes it was for height. But why try to hide it?

"He must have unscrewed it when he was in the Ladies' Room

and then not screwed it back on tightly on his way out.....but why would he want to cover it up?"

"He wasn't in there very long, that's for sure." said Lou "maybe he's got medicine in the hook or something and he went into the bathroom to take his medicine. Some old guys take a lot of medicine, ya know."

"True enough" said Muldoon "but again ....why try to hide the fact that the top part was not screwed in properly? And if it *is* his medicine...why stash it inside his cane...why not just carry it in his pocket?"

Then the click went off. The click in Muldoon's head that happened when he started to connect dots that no one else did. Maybe it wasn't medicine for him at all, he pondered. Maybe it was pills for other people.

"Good work, Lou" he said, saying nothing about his silent thoughts....nothing about the click. "I'm heading home...gotta check in on Mugsy...can I give you a lift?"

"No thanks, Muldoon. I'm going to stick around for awhile."

Muldoon motioned Patti-cake nearer and suggested that in light of Wanda's death and all, they take a rain check on their dinner. Patti-cake heartily agreed. "How about Saturday......the funeral will be over and things might be returning to normal." They set the date for Saturday at Muldoon's cabin.

Muldoon left. Lou slid to the back of the bar to look for a chance to use the Ladies' Room.

He was having clicks of his own.

Chapter Twenty-Six

Muldoon would get home to Mugsy in all good time but on his way out of The Belly Up he decided that he was going to pay Wally Skudnick a little visit. He remembered the way Lou showed him and by using the back roads he hoped he would not run into Peter Branderford. By the time he got there, the ambulance had, of course, left as had Peter and his squad car. There was no activity outside the building and no hint that earlier that day, a woman had been shot there three times in the chest and died. In just a few passing hours, it returned to what Barry the Gambler had described in The Belly Up as the place "where the poor people live."

Muldoon was getting ready to press the buzzer for Apartment 35 when a couple with a baby carriage was attempting to make their way out the door to the Building Unit. They pushed the door open a little bit and he held the door wide for them. The couple acknowledged his gesture with a nod and showed no suspicion when Muldoon let himself into the building as they made their way out.

It was easy enough for him to locate Apartment 35 and he knocked heavily on the door.

"Who is it?" barked the man on the inside

"Plumbers, Mr. Skudnick.....have to bleed your radiator." was

Muldoon's response

"Come back later…I'm busy now."

Muldoon pounded on the door this time. "We have to do it today! We have no time to come back."

The pounding must have worked because the sound of the lock being unlocked from the inside was like music to Muldoon's ears.

As soon as Wally opened the door, he tried to close it. He knew immediately that there were no plumbers standing outside his door. He didn't know who it was but he knew it was no plumber.

Muldoon shoved his way into the apartment and slammed the door behind him. Wally backed away with a frightful look on his face. At 5'3" he knew he was no match for this very fit man who stood in front of him who was at *least* 6 feet tall. And Wally was a skinny 5'3" at that.

"Who are you?" he said nervously as he backed his way into the living room.

Muldoon said nothing. Not a word. He just kept walking very slowly towards a putrid little man who he knew he could take out with one punch.

"Who are you?!!" screamed Wally "What do you want from me?? Are you one of Yevgrev's guys?? Leave me alone. I told him already that I was leaving town. Leave me alone!! Please don't hurt me. I told him that I'm leaving today and I ain't saying anything to anybody."

Bingo! Click. Click. Click….inside Muldoon's brain.

Muldoon walked closer to Wally. Close enough so that he could see beads of sweat profusely forming on Wally's forehead. They were beginning to run down the side of his face.

"You high on something, Wally?" said Muldoon menacingly "you seem to be working up quite a sweat there. You're not nervous about anything are you?"

He followed Wally behind the couch where Wally was trapped against the wall.....no means of escape except straight through Muldoon Frickey:Private Investigator. Wally Skudnick was dead in the water.

When he was staring Wally up and down he saw what was known on the force in the big city as "the sealer". It was on the floor behind the couch....a small sport bag with the force's logo on the side.....just like the one Ken said Peter Branderford always carried with him on his trips to the big city.

"Traveling kind of light, aren't you, Wally?"

Wanda's ex-husband, Paul's sorry excuse for a father was beginning to crumble. "Please don't do nothing to me.....I'm leaving....I tell ya I'm leaving....I told Yevgrev that.....let me go!!"

Muldoon reached his left arm out, grabbed Wally by the shirt and planted him right up against the wall.

"You listen real good now, Wally.....this is your *only* chance to listen real good....you understand me?"

Wally tried to shake his head up and down affirmatively as best he could with Muldoon's fist pressing so tightly against his throat.

"My name is Muldoon Frickey. If I find out that you have skipped town, I'll hunt you down and kill you myself. So, you'd best stay put."

He said nothing more than that. He didn't have to. He let Wally go and walked away while the tiny man slid to the floor holding his throat...gasping for breath.

He turned around just once ......just once before he opened the door to Apartment 35. "I mean that Wally.....I mean that as sure as I am standing here. I know how to find you and I have lots of friends who know how to do it, too. I'll hunt you down and pump three shots right through *your* sorry little chest."

Back at The Belly Up Lou found an opportunity to slip in to the Ladies' Room after the crowd had thinned out. Most had drunk their fill by now and heard their fill about what they thought happened to Wanda. Nobody left knowing any more real information about her death than they knew when they walked in a few hours ago. But they came in wearing their hearts on their sleeves and, sadly, left the same way.

Lou had never been in the Ladies' Room before and was surprised at how much bigger it was than the Men's. "Makes sense" he thought "they primp...we don't."

He was not sure what he was looking for and wasn't sure how to begin....maybe something out of the ordinary would pop up..... something that would entice Larry Lutursky to come in here with some regularity. He lifted the top of the tank to the toilet and didn't see anything in there except the pump and water.....nothing out of the ordinary in there. He opened the doors to the vanity and looked inside...felt his hand all around the bottom of the sink and had a close look at the drain pipe.

If there was anything amiss, his young, but highly trained plumber's eye would have seen it. He lifted the framed painting of the Eiffel Tower (which looked like it must have cost all of ten dollars) off the wall. There was nothing on the back but a lot of scotch tape marks but no rips in the brown paper backing to this "work of art". He made a mental note of that to tell Muldoon. He yanked at the front of the tampon dispenser, pulled it down towards him and hit paydirt. There was a small plastic bag filled with at least a dozen pills......they looked like ecstasy pills to Lou. He thought he would take them to show Muldoon but then thought better of it. He had no idea of how long they had been inside the dispenser but he did not want to tip off whoever was suppose to pick them up. He flipped the front of the dispenser up to close it and flushed the toilet, just to make it seem like he was in there doing anything but snooping around.

He walked back to the front of the bar and took his seat. There were fewer people left now than before he went into the Ladies' Room. He counted about five left sitting at the bar. Patti-cake asked him what he was going to have.

"Let me have a double shot of tequila." answered Lou

"A double?" said Patti-cake

"Yeah…It's been a long day….and if you don't mind my saying so, you look exhausted."

"I am" she replied "I'm cutting out early. I called Teddy and he'd said he'd be here in a few minutes. I want to go home and try to get away from all this talk of death and dying."

Lou agreed and said that it was a bad day, indeed, for their small town.

Chapter Twenty-Seven

Wally was completely unnerved by Muldoon's threat. He popped a few more valium from the sport bag behind the couch. It was loaded with pharmaceuticals of every kind and enough crack cocaine, Special K and ecstasy for half of Belleva County. He always popped valium, lots of it, when he was feeling unnerved. He wanted to make a telephone call to Yevgrev but he couldn't remember where he left his telephone number, so he popped another valium hoping that if he calmed down he'd be able to remember where the number was. He wanted to tell Yevgrev about Muldoon's visit. He wanted to tell somebody that he was scared shitless.

He didn't dare phone Peter Branderford – not after what happened in his apartment earlier. When Wanda got over to Wally's apartment, Peter was already there with Wally. Before she could even get a full sentence out of her mouth, Peter took Wally's gun and shot her three times at close range. Wally was already so high that he was barely functional.

"Don't worry about a thing you pill-popping freak" laughed Peter "I'll just say you shot her in self defense and that'll be the end of it. I'm the law around here. Nobody's going to question me." He wiped his prints off Wally's gun and told him to grab hold of it. There'd now be no question that the gun had the prints of Wally: the pill popper on it and not Peter Branderford: the cold-blooded murderer.

But now it was dusk and the scrawny pill popper was growing more paranoid with every hour. He was supposed to have left town by now but he kept thinking about Muldoon's threat to hunt him down and kill him. He was descending into a whirlpool of delusional madness that was being accelerated by his self-proscribed new combination of speed and valium. Finally, he made the rash decision to just get up and leave. "Just let that bastard try and find me" he boasted to himself, thinking of Muldoon. "I'll be in France before he even knows I'm gone." Wally had always wanted to go to France, but it was impossible to get a passport with his record. So, his plan was to sneak aboard an ocean liner bound for France. In his pea-brain, drug addled mind, all he thought he needed to do was drive down to the big city and get over to the piers. He managed to pull himself up off the floor and headed for the apartment door and his car parked on the street in front of his building......
but not before popping some more speed and another valium -- for the road.

When he finally made it down the three flights of stairs and outside to his car, he realized that he forgot to bring his car keys and his wallet. "I'll need my wallet in France" he smiled to himself as he headed back inside.

When he got to the first floor landing he heard the commotion of a few guys coming downstairs. He looked up but was in no condition to see who was coming towards him. The speed and valium had not done much to improve his eyesight.

Halfway up the second flight of stairs there were six angry, young, muscular Latino guys staring him down.

He tried to focus but he was having a difficult enough time just standing up straight.

"Blanco bastardo" said one of them.

"Droga detallista" hissed another as they all stepped slowly towards Wally.

"Pervertido" cried the biggest one.

"Asesino" said the one with the iron pipe as he brought it crashing onto Wally's neck.

"Tu matastes ami pequena hermana!!!!!" howled the youngest as he began bashing Wally's face in with crushing blow after crushing blow.

Deadly kicks to his ribs most likely punctured his lungs and whatever kidney function the pill popper had left was probably destroyed by multiple kicks to his lower back. One final punch to his face dislocated Wally's jaw and it hung loosely as the blood from his broken nose dripped into his open mouth.

They kicked him down to the first floor landing and the youngest bent down to whisper in Wally's ear, "Para Esperanza, fajina." They left him there.....breathing, but only just barely. They would leave the 911 call to some passerby.

Night had fallen by the time the ambulance unit received an anonymous 911 call. Wally was rushed to the emergency room of the local hospital in a physical condition that one of the ambulance attendants could only describe as "gross".

The medical staff, expert at seeing just about anything come into their emergency world, could do nothing to revive Wally to a conscious state. He had already fallen into a coma and his vital signs were barely registering. They had to list him as "extremely critical" but "nearly dead" would have been more appropriate.

Neither the ambulance attendants nor any of the emergency room nurses could find any kind of identification on the patient they now referred to as "John Doe".

"Somebody better call Chief Branderford and tell him we have a 'John Doe' about to expire." said Dr. Light, Head of Emergency Services.

Peter drove to the hospital two hours later, on his way home, and was shown the "John Doe" barely clinging to life.

Wally's face was so swollen, bruised and lacerated that he was unrecognizable. His jaw was stabilized but not re-set so it still hung causing his mouth to remain ajar. All of his front teeth had been knocked out and his lips were nearly three times their normal size. Both his eyes were black and blue and swollen completely shut. The hair on his head had to be shaved off so that a cranial drain could be inserted to relieve the pressure from a grossly swollen brain. His esophagus was busted in the attack and a tracheotomy was the only thing that allowed any air at all to move into his only remaining, but punctured, lung. His other lung had collapsed. Every single one of his ribs were broken and he was in renal failure.

Peter looked at Wally through the window of the Intensive Care Unit and legitimately did not know who it was. "Where did they pick him up?" he asked

When the nurse told him the address he just shook his head "Bad part of town over there" he said "a woman was shot in that building earlier today. The place ought to be condemned ....nothing but a bunch of low-lives and drug users over there anyway. When whoever this is finally dies, send him over to the morgue and they'll put him in a pauper's grave."

It could never have dawned on Peter that the body lying there was Wally Skudnick.

It could never have dawned on him because he would never have thought that Wally was anywhere except out of town heading to parts unknown – just like he told Yevgrev he was going to do. It would never have occurred to Peter that Wally would even think of defying Yevgrev.

But Peter could never have counted on a visit from Muldoon Frickey. Neither could he have ever anticipated a revenge attack from Esperanza's relatives.

All Peter could think of was Wally's promise to leave the sport bag full of drugs hidden behind the couch. "I'll go over tomorrow and get them" he said as he casually walked away from the unrecognizable, dying Wally Skudnick.

Chapter Twenty-Eight

Muldoon was out on his back deck having himself a nightcap while giving Mugsy a brief night-time brushing. "You are looking so fine these days, Mugsy old boy!" he said as he took a sip of his warm brandy. It had been an exceptionally long day for Muldoon and he was relishing his moments of peace and quiet with his dog. Mugsy was getting more responsive every day and had already gained twelve pounds since Muldoon brought him home from the pound. "You are one handsome dog, you know that?" he asked while he brushed the dog's hind quarters, almost expecting a response. He propped his shoeless feet up on the adjacent deck lounge and said "Let me ask you something, Mugsy..... let's see if you're smart enough to be the dog of a cracker-jack private investigator."

Mugsy cocked his head indicating that he was either confused, disinterested or wanted his own dish of warm brandy if Muldoon expected him to play "Private Investigator".

"Who would want Wanda Skudnick over at her ex-husband's apartment badly enough to try and lure her over there with some cockamamie story about Wally having inside information on her kid's death? Who would want her there in the first place? And who made the phone call.....doing, I might add, such a lousy job of disguising his voice that it was patently obvious, even to this grieving, hysterical mother, that the guy was disguising his voice. Who was it, I ask you my fine Irish Wolfhound, who set this wheel of death in motion?"

Mugsy was laying on the deck staring out at the lake. "Ah......so you don't know either, eh? Well...I am going to make a list of possible suspects because that's what cracker-jack private inspectors do, isn't it, old fella? I'll make up *my* list and you make up yours. Then we'll compare!" He got up from the lounge chair and went inside to get a pad and pen....and to give his brandy snifter another hefty refill. He was finally beginning to feel the tension of the day leave his body. When he walked into the kitchen, his cell phone, resting safely on the counter, began to ring.

"Muldoon Frickey here" he announced. The warm brandy made him forget to use his "officious voice" when he didn't recognize the telephone number being displayed.

"Hello. Mr. Frickey. This is Bill Lynch, director of the Saint Marie Anthony Cemetery. I'm sorry to be phoning so late...."

"Think nothing of it, Mr. Lynch....I'm still wide awake. What can I do for you?"

"Well.....as I understand it from our local funeral director, you will be paying for the headstone for Paul and Wanda Skudnick."

"That's right and I want the best looking head stone you have."

"That'll be no problem Mr. Frickey...no problem at all. But, I wanted to ask you two things....first: since you *are* paying for it, how do you want the inscriptions to read?"

"How do you mean, Mr. Lynch?"

"Well...it's customary to have the birth and death dates placed directly underneath the deceased's name and then some identifier directly underneath that....what sort of identifier did you want us to inscribe?"

"Oh.....I see...yes ...of course.....I forgot about that." He thought for a moment and then told Mr. Lynch what to use as identifiers.

"And anything across the top of the headstone?.....it's perfectly optional, of course but many relatives like to have the last name of the deceased in rather large letters...something along those lines."

Muldoon took a sip of brandy and thought carefully. Then he conveyed his wishes to Mr. Lynch. "That's very nice" was Lynch's response.

"And now just one more bit of business, if you don't mind."

"Not at all...go ahead" said Muldoon

"May I have your credit card number for payment?" he said in a detached manner

"Certainly" responded Muldoon as he obliged him with it "And Mr. Lynch....as I said...I want the best you have....I want this to look completely dignified and respectful."

"We won't disappoint, Mr. Frickey....rest assured....thank you kindly for your co-operation."

Pad, pen and re-filled brandy snifter in hand. Muldoon went back to his restful lounge on the deck thinking how strange it was to hear Mr. Lynch refer to Wanda as "the deceased". This time last night she was not deceased. Twenty-four hours ago she was still figuring out how to get through life without her beloved son, Paul.

Muldoon could only think of the classic song by one of his favorite singers, Dinah Washington "What a Difference a Day Makes".

Probably not a song he'd find on the jukebox at The Belly Up.

As he polished off the last of his warm brandy and brought Mugsy inside for the night he couldn't help but sing along with that song running around in his head.

"24 little hours….."

He was determined to get to the bottom of Wanda's death.

"and the difference is you…."

Chapter Twenty-Nine

By noon the next day, Muldoon and Mugsy were sitting in his office. Muldoon was finishing off a few new assignments from Gerry Dowling and Mugsy was sleeping on the floor. Muldoon was grateful for the additional work from Gerry and, in light of what he felt certain were the unusual circumstances surrounding Wanda's death, was seriously considering taking Gerry up on his offer of sending up a couple of agents from The Revona Group International -- just to help him keep an eye on things and certain people. "Self-defense, my ass" he thought "Wanda Skudnick couldn't hurt a fly. She was no threat to anybody including that puny little ex-husband of hers. There's _got_ to be something else going on here." There were lots of "clicks" going off in Muldoon's mind but none were igniting a believable scenario that would justify Peter Branderford's claim that Wally shot his ex-wife in self-defense.

If Muldoon knew what Wally knew about what really happened, he'd be off to Peter's like a shot. But he didn't know what Wally knew and was likely never to learn it from him inasmuch as the pill popper was stretched out in the hospital's ICU halfway between his pathetic station in life and his soon-to-be place in hell.

Try as he might, Muldoon simply could not determine who

on earth would want Wanda Skudnick dead. By all accounts she was very well thought of by her friends and co-workers. Who's way was she in? Who could she possibly be bothering? He was all but certain that Wally was somehow connected to Peter's trips to the big city by virtue of the sport bag that was laying on the floor behind the couch in Wally's apartment. It fit the description of the bag that Ken said Peter brought with him on all his trips. Muldoon was kicking himself for not opening the bag when he was in Wally's apartment. "I'll stake my reputation that it was probably jam filled with all sorts of drugs that Peter brought back with him."

He was trying to work the circle of facts back to Wanda but what he arrived at was mere conjecture and not any kind of conclusion. "Yevgrev *has* to be the supplier" he mused "and Peter's spreading the drugs around town…maybe throughout the county, too." Muldoon figured that Wally was most likely the "delivery boy" on the drugs. And then he remembered Larry Lutursky's "adjustable cane". Maybe it was Larry who was making the drops at The Belly Up and Wally was used for more distant points in the county.

But what did any of this have to do with Wanda?

Then the "click" went off. It was really more like an implosion. The click ran all the way down to Muldoon's toenails and back to his brain. Why hadn't he seen this before? He picked up the telephone immediately and dialed Gerry Dowling's number.

"Mr. Dowling's office. May I help you?" said the familiar voice

"Louise….hi…..it's Muldoon…..Muldoon Frickey….is your boss in?….it's kind of an emergency."

"Hello Muldoon…..Mr. Dowling's in the conference room with a client right now and I can't put you through….there's a few people in there with him and he said not to disturb him while the meeting was in progress."

Muldoon's brain was racing and asked Louise if she would just carry a written message into Gerry. "I guess I could do that" she replied "what's the message?"

"Write this, Louise……just exactly as I say it."

"Are you OK, Muldoon? You sound a bit edgy."

"The message should say this" he said not directly answering her question "I AM IN BIG TROUBLE. CALL ASAP."

The line was quiet. It seemed as if it had been disconnected. "Did you get that, Louise?"

"Yes" was her monosyllabic response "I'm going to bring it in right now….do you want to hold?"

"No. Just give him the message. I know Gerry. He'll call as fast as he can. Thanks, Louise."

Muldoon placed the receiver down slowly and gave the sleeping Musgy a tap "C'mon boy….we're going home." It was already two o'clock and Wanda's wake started in two hours. Muldoon had to get home, get out of his sweats, shave, shower and get dressed in his suit. He wanted to be there early so he could go over some details with the funeral director about how he wanted things to go smoothly from the funeral home to the church and, finally, to cemetery tomorrow.

He realized now that Wanda was never the real problem. But Muldoon knew that for Yevgrev and Peter, *he* was a sticky commodity. His prowess as a relentless investigator was well known to both of them. He determined that Wanda's death bore the familiar handiwork of Yevgrev and his orders were being executed by his own personal dirty cop, Peter Branderford.

Muldoon also knew now that Peter lied when he asked him in front of Wally's building what *kind* of work he was doing for Wanda. He knew all along. The question is *how* did he know? Who in this small town was feeding information to the Chief of

Police?

He knew now *why* Wanda was killed, but he still could not figure out *who* to point the finger at. He wanted to be certain. There
was no room for mistakes. Just like William Holden's character,
Sefton, in the movie "Stalag 17", Muldoon wanted to make sure
he fingered the right guy.

It was all too sad and clear now to Muldoon that Wanda
was just an expendable, innocent by-stander. The one they really
wanted out of the way was him -- because sooner or later they
knew he'd uncover Peter's drug connections to Yevgrev and tie
them both to Paul's death. But they were too wary of attempting
to take him out of the equation directly. Muldoon reasoned that
they must have thought by getting rid of Wanda, they'd also get
rid of him by ending his investigation into the truth behind Paul
Skudnick's drug related death. Wanda's death might even have
been a warning to Muldoon that he was next if he didn't back off.
The blood thirsty Russian and the dirty cop may have had the
idea that Wanda's death would scare Muldoon away.

"How wrong they are." Muldoon said while driving the half-
mile back to his cabin "How completely wrong they are."

_____

Almost before the sun rose that morning, Peter arrived at
Wally's apartment building. The tenants in his unit were still
sleeping and the small town's Chief of Police entered the building
unnoticed with the spare set of keys he demanded from Wally
when he first started to use him over two years ago as his drug
mule to every waiting user that called and pleaded for "just a little
bit." The door to Apartment 35 was unlocked and Peter went in
to look for his sport bag. The first thing he noticed was the lousy
clean-up job Wally was suppose to have done after Wanda's body
was carted away. There were still obvious blood spatters here and

there. He shrugged. "The landlord's going to have to paint the place anyway for the next tenant." Yevgrev made it clear to Wally that he was definitely not to return on penalty of his *own* death.

It didn't take Peter long to find the stash. He looked inside the bag and was mildly amused that the supply of valium and speed looked to be a little lighter than the rest of the drugs in the bag. "That little pill-popping freak" he said as he zipped up the bag. He was going to lock the apartment door on his way out but he decided to leave it the way he found it – carelessly unlocked. It was the way Wally left it yesterday when his drug-riddled delusions of grandeur made him think that he was on his way to France.

Peter still had no idea that the hospital had renamed the battered man with no identification, the unrecognizable Wally Skudnick "John Doe" All he cared about was that Wally appeared to have left town. Yevgrev would be happy, he thought.

"I know I am" he said as he walked to his squad car. He did not even notice that Wally's beat up old car was still parked across the street. "Nothing to worry about now."

Or so he thought.

Chapter Thirty

The funeral parlor was down the other side of the hill from the park where the two kids found Mugsy nearly beaten and starved to death. As he made his approach, Muldoon could see that there was already a long row of cars lining the east side of the park, closest to the funeral home. He also saw something else that he simply could not believe. Peter Branderford was ticketing all the cars that were park along the east side of the park. Parking tickets at a wake!!! Muldoon was incensed. He pulled his car in back of the long line of cars and hopped out.

Branderford saw him and shouted "If you park there Muldoon, you are going to get a $50 ticket for illegal parking."

He rushed up to Peter and shouted at him "What the hell do you think you're doing, Peter? There's a wake going on in there."

"I'm doing my job, buddy boy -- by the book. There's no parking along the east side here."

"The parking lot's probably full! What's the matter with you?"

Peter kept writing tickets. "Go in and tell your friends that they have ten minutes to move these cars or I'm having them towed. Tell them to get their grieving done and get going."

Muldoon turned away from Peter and headed back to his truck. He felt an anger welling up in him that would have raised his dead father from his grave. He opened the door to his truck and reached way in back of the seat for the brown paper bag that contained the leather dog leash that Kitty had to cut off of Mugsy's neck when they brought him into the pound. It had been stashed back there since the day Muldoon brought him home. He loosely wrapped it in circles and grabbed it tightly with his right fist.

Peter saw him walking back. "I mean it, Muldoon….you are no exception….I'm writing you a ticket if you don't move your truck."

Muldoon kept on walking straight toward him and stopped two feet in front of his face. "What are you, Peter? -- a police officer or a meter maid?"

"Don't piss me off, man…I'm the Chief of…"

Muldoon cut him short. "Wrong. Wrong. Wrong" he said through his bitterly clenched jaw "the rule is: Don't Piss _Me_ Off".

He held the dog leash up to Peter's face. "Recognize this?"

Before Peter could answer, Muldoon whipped him hard across the left side of his face. The rusted metal hook caught Peter's lip and it started to bleed. Peter stood there stunned. Before he could react, Muldoon came back across the right side of Peter's face with another hard whipping. This time the rusted hook caught Peter's upper lip and nostril. Both began to bleed immediately.

"What the…."

In the second it took Peter to try and complete his sentence, Muldoon brought the leash once more across the left side of his face. The force of this third blow opened his left nostril which began to bleed profusely and Peter stumbled backwards and fell to the ground.

Muldoon kicked him in the groin and jammed his right foot into Peter's chest.

"I know what you did you son-of-a bitch." Peter laid there trying to wipe the blood away from his mouth.

"You get your dog-beating, dirty cop sorry ass up and remove all these tickets and get away from this wake. I don't want to see you near here, near the funeral or anywhere near the cemetery. If I do, I am going to shove this dog leash down your corrupt throat."

Muldoon strode away towards the front door of the funeral parlor and Peter crawled away like a beaten dog.

The funeral home was packed to capacity. The funeral director had Wanda laid out in the largest room and two of the other, smaller rooms were being used for tables filled with coffee urns, cups and saucers, water bottles and plates filled with assorted small cakes and cookies. Soft, muted mingling at a wake was perfectly ordinary in this small town.

Muldoon detected the scent of rose bouquets and lilac bunches as soon as he walked in the front door. He saw Kitty and Doc in the front near the casket and made his way to them. He had no idea who half the people attending the wake were but they seemed to know who he was by virtue of all the polite nods and whispered "Thank You"s he heard on his way up to the casket.

He gave Kitty a hug and said "You've done a great job here, Kitty. Everything looks wonderful."

"I did it all for Wanda" was Kitty's reply.

"Hello, Mr. Frickey" said Kitty's son, Patrick, as he made his way over to shake Muldoon's hand "thanks a bunch for doing this for Mrs. Skudnick....and for Paul. I tweeted just about everyone I knew and they tweeted other people they knew."

"It sure worked....that Tweeting thing...it's a full house here!"

"And she sure deserves it" said Doc Carlin.

Kitty took Muldoon towards the back office of the funeral parlor to introduce him to the funeral director. On the way back she told Muldoon that when she went over to the Skudnick house to get some nice things for Wanda to be buried in, she found a will on the top of Wanda's piano. "She loved to play the piano....she was really good, too....she took it up in high school and kept at it for years and years."

"What about this will, Kitty? Is it a formal document?"

"Yes" she replied "I didn't know Wanda had a will....she never mentioned anything about it to me....which doesn't surprise me now that I've read the will."

"Why's that?" asked Muldoon

"She left everything she had, which is basically the house, all paid off, and its contents and a fully paid up life insurance policy to Paul. But there's a clause in the will that says if Paul died before her then everything goes to me."

Muldoon raised his eyebrows a bit.

"I never knew anything about this. The date on the will is about a month after her divorce became final.....and all this time she never spoke a word about it. I .....I...had no idea at all....I mean I don't even have a will myself."

"Where did you say you found the will?"

On top of her piano....it was an upright....and old piano....I remember when she bought it....it looked like a piece of junk but she scrubbed and scraped and really turned it into a nice piece of furniture....she loved to play it."

"Was there anything next to the will?....any other document... any letter...anything like that?' Wanda shook her head. "I don't know what to make of this, Muldoon."

"She must have known that there was going to be trouble if she went over to Wally's.....why else would she have set the will out in the open where anyone coming into the house would clearly have seen it."

"Do you think she had a premonition of her own death?" whispered Kitty "she was a big believer in psychics and déjà vu's and all that sort of stuff. Maybe she knew she was taking her life in her hands by going over there."

"I don't know about that, Kitty....I can't say...I don't follow any of that psychic stuff. I'm an investigator....I follow the facts.... and the facts tell me that Wanda was set up."

"Set up?,,,,by who?!!!"

"I'm still working on that. But believe me, I'll get to the bottom of it no matter what. But for the meantime, let's focus on this task before us of getting Wanda buried properly. I just want to tell you again what a great job you've done organizing this on short notice."

"Doc and Ken have been a great help and this guy here." The funeral director, Mr. Clark Boyle, just walked out of one of the small rooms over to Kitty and Muldoon.

"Clark" said Kitty "I'd like you to meet Muldoon Frickey."

Clark extended his hand "It's a pleasure Mr. Frickey..."

"Please call me Muldoon." The two of them walked into Clark's private office to conduct the expensive business of mounting a beautiful wake and funeral. Kitty re-joined Doc at the head of the casket to greet and thank people for coming.

Chapter Thirty-One

A fair sized crowd left the funeral home at 6:00 o'clock and made their way over to The Belly Up for a few drinks. Teddy was tending bar and there were no more than a few customers in there before the flow of mourners entered. He had just given Larry Lutursky another shot and a beer when the first few filtered in. On the way over, Lou told Muldoon about finding the ecstasy pills inside the tampon dispenser. They decided they would check the dispenser when they got to The Belly Up to see if the pills were still there.

When Muldoon saw Larry Lutursky sitting at the end of the bar, he finally fit him perfectly into the drug delivery puzzle that included Yevgrev, Peter Branderford and Wally Skudnick. He decided that Larry had to be the smallest link in this drug operation because he was always inside The Belly Up – always sitting there at the dark end of the bar.

Then it hit him.....*always sitting in The Belly Up.*

It was Larry.....Larry was the stooge. It *had* to be him. Muldoon became certain of it the more he thought about it. Everytime Muldoon was in the bar talking about the investigation to Patti-cake, Teddy or Lou.....Larry Lutursky was sitting there saying nothing but hearing everything. Everything. He was the one feeding information to Peter Branderford.

He peddled Peter's drug and gave him information. The least likely candidate was the biggest snitch in town.

Muldoon bought Patti-cake a vodka and cranberry juice and got himself a Sam Adams beer. He set them down at the table in the front of the bar where they were joined by Kitty and Doc. Muldoon excused himself for a minute and motioned for Lou to join him at the back of the bar so they could get into the Ladies' Room when it was not occupied.

"I don't think they're still going to be inside the dispenser" said Lou

"You're probably right" answered Muldoon "it wouldn't make sense to make a drop to be picked up the next day or the day after. People who want their drugs want them right away......no waiting. But I see Lutursky sitting over there....he was here when we walked in....I wouldn't be surprised if there wasn't another bag of drugs in there.....a different one than what you discovered yesterday."

Pietro saw Muldoon standing by the door to the Ladies' Room and walked up to say hello. "I didn't get a chance at the funeral home to thank you for what you are doing for Wanda. Ken and Doc told me all about it.....incredibly generous of you."

Muldoon thanked him and took the opportunity right then and there to tell him, in whispered tones, that it looked very much like his Ladies' Room was being used as a place for drug drops. Lou described to Pietro how and where he found a small bag of drugs in there yesterday. "I think this has been going on for awhile." said Muldoon.

"Who's doing this?" asked Pietro

Lou shrugged "I don't know....can't say for certain."

"Let's just say we have our suspicions" said Muldoon. He reached out for the doorknob to the Ladies' Room to open the door but at the last second turned his shoulder towards Larry Lutursky and shouted just loud enough to make Larry very uncomfortable "Hey pal....you don't need to use the Ladies' Room just now do you? I know you prefer it to the men's toilet.....I just want to go in here for a minute, if that's OK with you....but I'll be glad to wait for you if you really need to use it."

Larry remained motionless on his bar stool.

Lou, Muldoon and Pietro went in and the door closed behind them. Once inside Lou grabbed the front of the tampon dispenser and pull it down as though he was going to re-stock it and sure enough there were two packets of pills – looked more like Vicodin than ecstasy – taped to the inside of the metal front.

"That's not the packet I saw in there yesterday." said Lou

"I can't believe this" said Pietro. He looked positively dejected. Lou also showed him all the tape marks on the back of the painting of the Eiffel Tower.

"From the number of tape marks on the back here, it looks like whoever was bringing the drugs in here must have thought the back of the painting was getting too obvious for their "non-clients" and they switched to the more secure drop point inside this tampon dispenser." explained Muldoon

"I just can't believe this" Pietro said with exasperation "my father would be rolling over in his grave if he knew drugs were being exchanged in The Belly Up."

Muldoon opened the door so they could exit and said "I'll tell you who I think is doing this, Pietro, and he's sitting right there."

But, he wasn't. He wasn't sitting anywhere in the bar. Larry Lutursky was gone....making his quick, unannounced exit, as usual.

"I can't prove my theory exactly......not right now at least" said Muldoon to Pietro "but I've made a really good educated guess that Larry is making the drug drops."

"I'm sick over this" said Pietro "this is not the kind of bar I want to be known as running. This has just been a local watering hole for more than 60 years. I'll sell it before I let it become an embarrassment to my family."

"I don't think anybody wants you to sell it, Pietro" said Lou "especially your Saturday night customers….it's a lot of fun in here…..people my age in town look forward to a good Saturday night at The Belly Up!"

"This is a travesty" replied Pietro "I can't have drugs in my father's bar."

Muldoon offered a suggestion. "If my theory is correct…..and I'm pretty sure it is…why don't you first eliminate the drop points in the Ladies' Room?"

"Yeah!" added Lou "I don't think anyone's going to miss that painting of the Eiffel Tower!! And so what if you take the tampon dispenser out? Women carry their own these days anyway."

"Lou's right, Pietro…..Larry is going to be surprised the next time he goes in the Ladies' Room and there's no safe place for him to leave his drugs.

"If I ever see that scumbag go into the Ladies' Room again, I'll crack his skull!!"

Pietro went downstairs to get the tools to remove the tampon dispenser and on his way tossed the painting of the Eiffel Tower in the big trash bin outside in the parking lot.

Muldoon re-joined Patti-cake, Doc and Kitty at the front of the bar while Lou said his good-byes for the evening "See you all tomorrow at the funeral mass."

———————————————

"You said there'd be no trouble!! You said this would be easy money and nobody would ever catch on!! Now I got this investigator smellin' blood and I ain't gonna be no sittin' duck for anybody! I ain't doin' this no more!"

Peter was in no mood to negotiate with Larry. He was nursing his fat lip and swollen nose courtesy of Muldoon and he was in a particularly foul mood. He grabbed the seventy-eight year old reprobate by his shirt and shoved him into the only sitting chair that Larry had in his one-room, dingy apartment.

"You have been making easy money on these drops for almost two and a half years so I don't want to hear any bitching or moaning from you....you pathetic old fuck! And you don't ever tell me what you are going to do....I tell _you_!" he screamed at him. "You are going to keep making these drops until I tell you to stop... not before...if I hear any more complaints from you, I'll cut your wrinkled old throat!"

"You can't make me...."

Peter grabbed Larry by the hair on the back of his head "Listen real good here....I can make you do anything I want you to do. Don't forget who I am. If I feel like it, I will arrest you on drug possession and you will spend whatever is left of your miserable, sorry life in jail. I can beat the shit out of you or I can kill you. I have a lot of options, you fucking moron.......*you*, on the other hand, have only one.....and that is to do *exactly* what I tell you to do whenever I tell you to do it!"

"That investigator is on to me......I'm sure he's figured out what's goin' on....I don't know how, but he's figured it out."

"Leave him to me...he's no concern of yours. I will take care of him."

After reporting to Yevgrev what happened in the park near the funeral home, Yevgrev gave Peter the order: "Kill him. I don't care how you do it but get it done by the weekend. End it."

Peter threw the sport bag filled with drugs on the floor and kicked it over to Larry and told him what the next drop was suppose to contain.

"Listen, Chief.....I don't want to take no money....I'll do the drops but I don't want to take the buy money....Wally always did that.....why can't....."

Peter cut him off again "I'm already sick of looking at you and listening to you. Yevgrev's men are taking the money....that's none of your business....you'll get paid the same way you have been ....cash at the end of every week so shut up and be grateful for what we give you, you hear?"

Larry nodded and asked when the next drop was supposed to take place.

"Make it tomorrow right after the bar opens. Hide that sport bag someplace, too. If you lose it, the next knock you'll hear on your door will be Yevgrev's very unhappy, heavily armed men."

"Why can't Wally do this?" Larry whimpered

"Wally's out of town for a while" was all Peter wanted to volunteer as he left Larry's apartment "it's tag now and you're *it*."

———————————

Muldoon walked Patti-cake to her car after they finished their drinks at The Belly Up.

"Say, Patti-cake, why don't I pick you up tomorrow morning on my way to the church? I can drive you home after the burial at the cemetery."

"That'll be fine, thanks Muldoon. I'm not going to feel much like driving myself. And by the way....when we're outside the bar, would you mind terribly if I asked you to call me by my real name?"

Muldoon was a bit taken back. He had not known her by any other name than Patti-cake. "I'm sorry" he said "I just thought that was your nickname....you know...for Patricia or something like that."

"It's what the customers started calling me when I first started tending bar in The Belly Up. You're right, tho.... it is a sort of nickname, but it's not short for Patricia or anything like that."

"I apologize.....I didn't mean to cause any offense."

"Oh....none taken" she replied "none at all....but outside of the bar, I'd just as soon have you call me by my real name."

There was an awkward moment of silence until Muldoon smiled and said "Well....OK....what *is* your name?"

She let a moment pass while the outside corners of her mouth turned ever so slightly upwards into the hint of a pretty smile. "It's Helenka."

Her little-bitty smile was lassoing little-bitty ropes around Muldoon's heart and all he could say in response was "That's a beautiful name." What he really was thinking was that it was a beautiful Greek name for a beautiful Greek woman. Then he said it aloud...returning her smile "Helenka......it suits you beautifully."

"It means 'light'." she added with a quiet sense of pride

Muldoon said no more......except he thought to himself.... "of course it does..... 'Let there be light'......how perfect.

Helenka gave him the address and directions to her house and said she'd be ready and waiting in time for the 10:00 am funeral mass.

Chapter Thirty-Two

Kitty decided not to have a procession of cars from the funeral home to the church. Muldoon told her that whatever she wanted was just fine with him. Since there were no direct living relatives, she didn't see the need for the protocol of shuffling people into cars and then right back out of them a mile down the road at the church. Everyone knew that the funeral mass would start at 10:00 am and they would gather there. Kitty and her son Patrick rode in the hearse from the funeral home. She didn't want Wanda to be alone in the back of the hearse as though she had no friends. It was, in fact, just the opposite. Nearly everyone who was at the wake attended the mass at the Church of The Good Shepherd. Fr. Reid, the kindly and beloved pastor of the parish was officiating at the mass. He was seventy-two years old and had administered all of the major sacraments to nearly all of the people now waiting in his church for the casket of Wanda Skudnick to be rolled up the aisle by six senior altar boys acting as pall bearers. He baptized Wanda thirty-seven years ago, married her, said the funeral mass for her son, Paul and now was about to begin the blessing over her casket draped with lilies of the valley and forget-me-nots.

There was an obvious numbness in the audible liturgical responses given by the congregation. It was as though, until just now, the horror, mystery, sadness and grief over Wanda's death was beginning to register too closely with them. The hearse, the closed casket, too many lit candles in a poorly lit church, the somber and funereal pace of Fr. Reid's officiating and the haunting version of "Ave Maria" played into the church's speaker system had a whisking effect on their emotions. It left holes in their hearts, large and small. Her death was too immediate and without warning. No one was ever going to see Wanda again. Real sadness was the order of the day and it showed on all their faces.

Kitty stepped up to the altar podium to read Psalm 23 and burst into sobs when she reached the last line "surely goodness and mercy will follow me all the days of my life". Muldoon had to escort her back to her pew. Kitty knew along with many others in the church that "goodness and mercy" were surely things that Wanda believed in but "trouble and turmoil" were the things that always followed her best friend.

The real blessing-in-disguise was when Fr. Reid gave the final blessing and the altar boys began to roll Wanda's casket out to the waiting hearse. The congregation was reaching a breaking point and they needed to leave.

The drive to Saint Marie Anthony cemetery was only two and a half miles past the far side of the park and up a hill that over-looked parts of the small town on one side and the River Pawtonka on the other. Muldoon was very pleased that the engraving on the headstone was completed so quickly and that Paul's casket had been exhumed for re-burial next to his mother. When Wanda's casket was set on the cross-frame over her grave, the image of mother and son entombed as such was too much for the mourners to bear. The large crowd of Paul's friends from high school wept openly and the adults were stunned into a new recognition of the fragility of life altogether.

It was the first time any of them had seen the beautiful head-stone and were deeply moved by what Muldoon had engraved on it.

The identifier underneath Paul's name and dates of birth and death said simply "loving son". Wanda's said "loving mother". No one could question that sentiment -- not for eternity. The name "SKUDNICK" was engraved in capital letters in the center of the headstone and along the top was something that Muldoon especially wanted there. That engraving read: "Let justice be done, though the heavens fall". It was a reminder to everyone that there was unfinished business here.

Slowly the crowd dispersed so the cemetery workers could start to carry out their duties.

It was all over by Noon.

As they walked down the hill towards his parked truck, Patticake grabbed ahold tightly of Muldoon's arm. "I'm proud to know you Muldoon Frickey" she said as she dabbed away her tears "that was a beautiful service and that headstone is more than just a grave marker. It tells you who really is buried there. It's just gorgeous."

He put his arm around her and sweetly kissed the top of her head. "Thanks Helenka. I'm glad you liked it. That means something to me."

There was a general agreement that anyone who didn't have to get to work would meet at The Belly Up at 12:30pm for a few drinks of consolation. Teddy was going to be on the bar as Patticake had arranged with Pietro to take the whole day off.

At 12:15 pm over at the local hospital's ICU, Wally Skudnick flatlined. While one of the nurses disconnected all the tubes, an attending physician was called in to officially pronounce "John Doe" dead. "Better call the morgue" said the doctor "they'll come over and remove him and put him in a pauper's grave."

Ken and Lou were the first ones to walk into The Belly Up after the burial at the cemetery. They both agreed that Paul and Wanda had been properly laid to rest with dignity.

"It makes me feel better just knowing that they've been buried like the decent folks they were." said Ken

"Yeah....it was a class operation from beginning to end. Muldoon sure did right by them. He's a classy guy." said Lou

"He's definitely that" answered Ken "unlike that utterly class-less heap at the end of the bar there."

Ken was talking about Larry Lutursky, who was the only other customer in the bar other than Carl when Ken and Lou walked in. Ken whispered to Teddy "How long has that bum been in here?"

Teddy could have easily asked "Which one?" but Ken's feelings towards Larry were well known so Teddy was pretty sure who he was asking about.

"He came in right after I opened. I unlocked the back door and he was standing there. I gave him his first shot and beer and then went downstairs to bring up a few cases for the cooler."

"Was Carl in here, too?" Lou wanted to know

"No. But, Carl was sitting at the bar when I came back up with the cases. Why do you ask?"

"Just curious" said Lou as he walked back towards the Ladies' Room. Larry was eyeing him all the way.

"You having something to drink, Lou?" Teddy asked

"Sure.....my usual and one for Ken" he said as he knocked on the Ladies' Room door. No answer. "Hmmmmm" he said quite loudly "must be empty."

Lou opened the door and held it opened as he said just as loudly "Gee....it looks like Pietro took down the tampon dispenser!" Larry was grabbing tightly ahold of his empty shot glass.

"And that beautiful painting of the Eiffel Tower is gone too!!"

he said mockingly as he headed slowly back to the front of the bar. "Gosh Almighty" he said snidely glancing at Larry "just when you think things are going good – somebody up and changes it. Boy, I hate that….don't you Ken?"

Larry got up with enough force that his bar stool fell to the floor. He picked up his shot glass and threw it at the back of Lou's head, hitting him dead center.

Lou made a flying dash towards Larry to crush him that was interrupted only because Teddy leapt over the bar and landed in between them.

"Easy Lou…easy…don't kill him…..he's seventy-eight years old….Branderford would be more than happy to arrest you." Ken ran around all of them and opened up the back door to the bar because he knew what was coming next. Teddy was having a tough time calming Lou down. He was enraged and his temper was rising as fast as the welt on the back of his head.

"C'mon Lou….let me put some ice on that before you get a headache that you can't wash away with beer."

"Get him out of here before I kill him!!! Get him out!" screamed Lou

Teddy was still trying to keep Lou at a distance and turned to Ken and said "Ken…do the honors, will you?"

"Nothing would give me greater pleasure" said the tall helicopter pilot "I've been waiting years for this."

"And take his cane!" yelled Lou

Larry went out the back door with a great shove from Ken and sniped when Ken tried to grab his cane "You ain't taking nothin' from me, you prick."

"Hit the road, buddy….and don't come back." warned Ken

Teddy wrapped some bar ice up in a towel and gave it to Lou to press against the back of his head. "You'll be alright…..he's seventy-eight years old….he throws like a girl. Drink your beer…

next one's on the house."

Carl sat there dumbfounded at the quick turn of events and finally said "I never liked that son-of-a bitch. I lent him $100 about thirty-five years ago and he never paid me back. .....never liked him. He's always been a rotten son-of-a bitch."

Ken laughed at the notion of Carl even being able to remember an outstanding debt of thirty-five years. "He's rotten to the core, isn't he Carl?" joked Ken

"He's nothin' but a first class bum....lemme tell ya!"

The bar filled up pretty quickly after that with people who had been at the cemetery. Word spread pretty quickly about what Larry did to Lou.

Not a whole lot of nice words were said about Larry Lutursky that afternoon.

Chapter Thirty-Three

Muldoon had an idea on the way over to The Belly Up from the cemetery. "Say, Helenka…as long as you have the rest of the day off, why don't we be spontaneous here and have our dinner out at the cabin tonight instead of Saturday? Might be a good way for us to take our minds away from the gloom of the day. I'll pop into the German Meat Market and get chicken to barbecue on the grill out on the deck and I have plenty of stuff and fixin's in my kitchen for a salad and a couple of side dishes. It's still early and we can relax a bit before I rustle up the food. Sound like a good idea to you?"

"An early dinner sounds nice, Muldoon. Let's do it. I could use a little down time from the bar and letting you do all the work sounds like a *very* relaxing time to me!" she joked

Muldoon pulled into the parking lot and said "I won't be a tic" and added "chicken's OK with you?" She nodded.

When he returned he said he was anxious to get back to the cabin and let Mugsy run around the back yard. Helenka asked him if he had any greek olives.

"Hmmm….no….I don't think so."

"Any feta cheese?"

"I'm *sure* I don't have any of that" he responded "why do you ask?"

"How can you offer a Greek girl a Greek salad with dinner if you don't have any greek olives or feta cheese?"

He shrugged not knowing what to say.

She looked at him with a teasing, mock disapproval and said "We'd better make a quick stop at my house before we head out to the cabin. Sounds like I should bring a few things out to help your menu along!! And, I can get out of this dress and into something more 'everyday'".

As Muldoon made the correct left and right turns to get over to Helenka's house, all he could remember hearing was "get out of this dress." It was a pre-occupying thought and he needed to concentrate on the road or else they'd never make it out to the cabin.

As he pulled in to her driveway, she hopped out and said "Now, I'm the one who'll be out in a tic!" She did not invite him in. He watched her walk into the house and tried to calculate how fast he could drive out to the cabin without flipping his truck over. "What a beautiful woman she is" was his driving thought.

She was not inside her house for more than ten minutes when she walked out with a grocery bag filled with all sorts of stuff and a pastry box filled with God-knows-what. In whatever time was left after she packed up the food, she had managed to lose the black ribbon she wore at the funeral to tie her hair back, put on different colored lip-stick and change into a white cotton blouse tucked into a killer pair of relaxed-fit blue jeans rolled up at the ankle and a white and blue pair of cotton deck shoes.

Muldoon saw her and let out the kind of whimper that a thirteen-year old boy lets out when he's just seen his first Playboy centerfold.

He reached over and opened the passenger door from the inside. "You are a quick change artist!" he said taking the bag and pastry box from her.

"Nothing to it, really"

"What's in the bag?"

"Oh….just a few things to help you along with for the salad and the chicken."

"The chicken, too?" he asked

"Sure. I'll bet you don't know how to barbeque a chicken Greek style, do you?'

"Oh….I'm getting the feeling that I don't know very much right now." he answered

"What's in the box?" he asked

"Baklava" she said

"Baklava?"

"Yes…..I always have some baklava in my house….it's for desert."

"I know at least *that* much" said Muldoon

"Because…..if you'll remember…..I told you that *I* am not desert!" she said with that damn Melina Mercouri laugh of hers.

Muldoon smiled and turned the ignition on and adjusted the rear view mirror "Yes, Helenka…..I heard you the first time you said it."

She winked at him and said "Careful as you back out."

Peter Branderford did not like the telephone call he received from Larry Lutursky. He knew that Yevgrev would like what Larry said to Peter even less. The Belly Up had been a convenient, low-maintenance drop point for Yevgrev's drugs for more than two years now. "Easy money" he always said to Branderford "and it's your responsibility to keep it that way."

And that's the way it was since just after Peter replaced Nick Spalata as Chief of Police. Wally Skudnick and Larry Lutursky were the perfect "mules". Nobody would have ever suspected them of being anything but low-life, reprobate drunks.

Everything ran just as smooth as silk until Muldoon Frickey started investigating the death of Paul Skudnick.

But neither Paul, nor his mother Wanda were the real problems now. They were dead and buried. Even Wally Skudnick was dead – although no one actually knew it or, more importantly, probably would not have cared.

No.....it was Muldoon who was the last remaining problem. Or at least that's what Peter thought until he got Larry's telephone call.

"They know!!!" he screamed into the phone "I'm sure of it now. I can't go back in there with any drugs. They've figured it all out. Both the painting and the tampon dispenser have been taken out of the bathroom."

"Shut up and stop screaming in my ear" snapped Peter

"I don't know what to do.....they threw me out.....I can't go back there...you have to get someone else..."

"I told you before, you idiot....*you're it!*"

"I'm tellin' you that the bartender made me leave."

"Don't worry about him....his shift ends at 7 o'clock tonight. You're going back there after he leaves. Yevgrev made a deal to have another drop in there tonight and you're the one who's going to make it."

"It's not safe.....there's bound to be..."

"I told you to shut up.....don't worry about anything being 'safe'.....I'll be there."

"Then why don't *you* make the drop!!" screamed Larry

All Peter could think of right then and there was that Larry was lucky he was on the other end of a telephone connection otherwise he'd be on the receiving end of Peter's fist.

"Listen to me, you useless drunk....*you* never tell me what to do ....*I* tell you what to do.....don't ever say something as stupid as that again or I'll cut your throat!!"

The very tone of Peter's menacing threat told Larry that he meant business and he had no reply.

"You meet me in the back of the bar at midnight and I will tell you exactly what to do." With that order clearly made, Peter ended the conversation and called Yevgrev and told him everything.

"You know what to do." was Yevgrev's only response before he hung up.

Chapter Thirty-Four

Mugsy took quite a shine to Helenka. It was instantaneous and Muldoon was as surprised as he was amused. He opened a bottle of wine and let it set on the back deck to breathe while he walked Mugsy and Helenka down to the water's edge.

"I used to come fishing up here a lot with my father....that's why I chose this place after I came back from my travels." he told her

"It's beautiful, Muldoon and that is a mighty fine looking canoe you've got tied up there. It looks like an original."

"It's practically my pride and joy....aside from my truck." he joked

"And Mugsy here!" she added

"Yeah.....of course....but Mugsy's really in a class all by himself."

Muldoon liked being at his cabin with Helenka. He liked leaving "Patti-cake" back at The Belly Up. Helenka was different and he liked not having to vie for her attention with any number of other bar patrons. He enjoyed having quality time with this quality woman.

He poured them both a nice full glass of red wine when they returned to the deck.

"You still look a little troubled from the mass and burial." said

Helenka

"It's not so much that" replied Muldoon "it's Wanda's death that really bothers me."

Helenka said that it was a travesty the way Wanda was killed by her ex-husband. Neither she nor Muldoon or anyone, for that matter, knew that Peter Branderford was the real murderer. Only Wally knew – and he was dead.

"It's a terrible thing, no doubt" agreed Muldoon "but…" then he paused

"But what" she asked

"But….I think I may have been that cause of it."

"That doesn't make any sense to me Muldoon. How?…or why would you be the cause of Wanda's death?"

"There's a lot you don't know Helenka……a lot."

"Well….looks like there's plenty of wine and it's still early. I have plenty of time. Why don't you tell me."

She was irresistible. Muldoon knew in that moment that he did not have to test her or try and pump her for information. He knew just by the special look in her eye that she could be trusted.

And so he told her. Everything.

An hour and several wine glass re-fills later, Muldoon finished telling his tale. Helenka got up from the deck chair.

"So….what do you think?' he asked

"I think we should go into the kitchen and start getting some of our early dinner prepared…..and I think you need to relax a bit….I always find that cooking is a good way to relax. Let's go."

Muldoon followed her into the kitchen with Mugsy in tow.

Instinctively she started pulling out the right pots and pans and dishes to use. Muldoon opened the fridge and started bringing out the chicken and other foods for the barbeque. Helenka started to put all the things she brought from her home out of the bag and place on the kitchen counter. She stopped for a moment and he noticed it.

"Something wrong?" he asked

"I'll just say this, Muldoon before I comment on anything else you've just told me because I have to take a little time to digest it. But, what I'll say is this: I don't like Peter Branderford and I never did. I don't really know anyone in town who does like him. I've never had any trouble with him, mind you. But I never liked the cut of him and I think you did the right thing in calling your friend Gerry in the big city for some protection. I think Peter is a dangerous man. I see it in his eyes all the time. And that's all I'm going to say right now."

Peter decided that no response was necessary. Helenka just spoke her mind and that was sufficient for him.

"So…" she said after a quiet moment passed between the two of them "you have any nice music here you can play while we cook?"

"Oh…sure…yeah… plenty of music in the cabin….what's your preference?'

"Have you got any Ella Fitzgerald?"

He smiled that devilish Muldoon Frickey smile of his. "Ella?…. are you kidding…have I *ever* got Ella!!"

He went into the living room to load a few Ella cds into his stereo. "Ella!!" he whispered to Mugsy who followed him into the living room "I can't believe the first music she asked for was Ella. This woman is too perfect for words, Mugsy 'ol boy!!"

In the kitchen, Helenka thought to herself as she sifted through her spices "Gotta love a man who loves Ella."

Larry was getting very uptight…..very nervous about his midnight meeting with Peter. He knew The Belly Up would be packed. It always was on Saturday nights….lots of carousing and drinking and it was karaoke night, too. Too many drunks trying to sing like Faith Hill or Tim McGraw. It was always a very loud, very long night and whenever Larry made any previous drops in there on Saturday nights, it was always well before the karaoke massacre started – not when it was at its midnight hour fever pitch. He was looking for a way out of this and saw nothing but an eventual, meek compliance with Peter's order.

Then, he decided to phone Wally at the telephone number Wally gave him to use "only in the case of dire emergency". It rang and rang and rang. Larry called the number a few times and let it ring and ring. There was never any answer. Had he, too, known what happened to Wally he'd have realized that it's impossible to answer your cell phone from your grave --- any grave --- pauper's or otherwise.

He entertained for a moment -- a very brief moment -- the idea of not going to the midnight meet-up but he knew that Peter would track him down and probably kill him. Larry began to regret that he ever got involved with "that treacherous fucker" in the first place. But now he had nowhere to go and no one to whom he could turn. He was suffering the fate of a broken-down, poor, lonely and friendless alcoholic. He was a man completely alone with his own fate. It was a destiny of his own making. He realized that he had no choice but to meet Peter at midnight behind The Belly Up. Resigning himself to this fact, Larry began to drink -- very heavily.

The barbeque/dinner whipped up by Chef Helenka and Chef Muldoon was just a hair's breath short of a real feast. Even Mugsy could tell that the both of them were having a good time in each other's company. Then it came time for desert.

Muldoon began to clear the dishes from the deck table and

bring them into the kitchen. Helenka brought in the wine bottles, of which there were several, and the wine glasses and set them on the counter.

"Why don't we bring the party into the living room, Helenka?" he suggested. "It's starting to get kind of cool out there with the night breeze coming off lake. I can stoke up a fire real quick and maybe put on an old movie while we have our baklava?"

Helenka looked at her watch. It was later than she thought but too early to call it a night. "OK.....which old movie goes good with baklava?"

If it were up to Muldoon he'd have put "Play Misty for Me" on...or maybe "Serpico" but they weren't exactly "chick flicks". His mind was racing through his mental bank of all his old favorites and realized there were too few "chick flicks" to screen and decided to find some neutral ground with an old James Stewart movie "Harvey".

"Ever see it?' he shouted from the living room as he lit the fire.

"Nope" she answered back as she loaded the dishwasher.

"It's about this guy who likes to drink a martini or two and has a six foot tall invisible rabbit as his best friend."

"Sounds like an afternoon at The Belly Up" she said with a laugh "is it any good?"

"It's good for a few laughs....it's an old black and white film." he said as he walked back in to the kitchen.

In the time that it had taken him to load the logs into the fireplace, light the fire, pick out the dvd and settle Mugsy onto his comfy mattress next to the hearth, Helenka had rinsed the dishes, loaded them into the dishwasher, found two small desert plates and forks and set out the "Baklava for Two".

"Is there anything you *can't* do?" he asked

"Well....I can't seem to find any nice after-dinner liqueur to go with the desert." she teased.

Muldoon waltzed over to the small cabinet next to the fridge and yanked out a little-used bottle of Disaronno Amaretto. He held it high and sauntered back to the counter and announced "Made from a secret formula --- unchanged since the year 1525."

Helenka smiled "Not much call for it at the bar......and now for some demi-tasse glasses?"

Muldoon reached under the kitchen sink and brought out two shot glasses....one from Greece and one from Ireland. "I got these along the way in my travels!!"

"Shot glasses?"

"Yep....special ones, tho! We can pretend they're demi-tasse glasses with stems...can't have everything. Besides, who needs demi-tasse glasses?...you're not trying to get me drunk are you, Miss??"

"Not on amaretto!!" she said "*you* might wind up being desert!!"

She picked up the forks and the two plates of baklava and headed for the living room. "Why don't you grab some napkins and that "special" glass wear of yours?"

Muldoon complied, grabbed the bottle of amaretto and thought about volunteering to become the desert.

Chapter Thirty-Five

Peter was in the darkest corner of the parking lot in back of The Belly Up waiting for Larry. He parked his squad car in the school yard a block away where no one would bother with it – or even notice it for that matter. The music was so loud inside the bar that he felt like he was going to have to yell for Larry to hear what he had to say and he did not want to bring any attention to himself. He was getting antsy waiting for Larry and when he became antsy, he became more irascible than usual.

Larry had two strikes against him before he even got to the parking lot. Number one was that Peter did not want to be there. A midnight meeting was a great inconvenience for him. Number two was that he didn't like Larry. No one did. But Peter learned very easily more than two years ago what a drunk like Larry would do for a little extra cash. So, he started to use him to make the drops inside The Belly Up....all with no problems until Muldoon Frickey showed up.

Peter's mood was becoming increasingly foul by the time he saw Larry make his way into the parking lot. Even with his cane in hand, he was walking with great difficulty. He was propping himself up against the brick wall that lined the back of the parking lot and mumbling something to himself that Peter could not make out. Larry was about to turn in the direction of the back door when Peter quickly darted the few yards that separated them and grabbed Larry by the back of his shirt and shoved him into the corner where he had been waiting. Taken by surprise as he was, Larry nearly let out a yelp before he recognized who it was that had just man-handled him into a corner.

Peter had to turn his head away before he gagged on the putrid and overwhelming smell of booze that hung over Larry like a gathering storm. He tried in vain to wrestle out of Peter's grip but he was too far gone with whatever amounts of liquor he had been guzzling to put up anything close to an effective resistance. Larry was stone cold drunk and Peter's anger level just reached its boiling point.

"You stinking old drunk" Peter said as he shoved Larry to the ground. "How to you expect to go in there and make a drop!"

Larry was almost too drunk to talk. "Answer me!!" said Peter as he shoved his boot onto Larry's stomach.

"Ain't." was all he could manage in reply

"What do you mean 'ain't'" Peter demanded as he pulled Larry to his feet using one arm and pressed him against the brick wall.

"Ain't doin' it…..keep your money….I ain't goin' in there."

Peter jammed Larry in the back of his head with a closed fist. "You don't get to decide that. I'm the one who decides that." Peter was no longer threatening Larry. The second smash to the back of his head was proof enough of that. At this stage Larry was of no more use to Peter than one of his drug-addicted snitches in the big city used to be.

"Go in there yourself, asshole" was Larry's defiant answer.

It was the last answer Larry Lutursky would ever make. They were the last words he would ever utter.

Enraged, Peter reached into his back pocket and pulled out a six inch serrated-edged knife that normally would have been used to gut fish and ran it deep and hard straight across Larry's scraggly neck nearly severing it from his body. Blood spurted everywhere. Peter dropped the profusely bleeding drunk to the ground and knelt down next to him. "What you 'ain't', you dead-ass drunk, is walking out of this parking lot alive!" He took the knife and for good measure ran it right along the thirty nine-year old scar on Larry's face that he got in a fight in the parking lot outside The Belly Up. It ripped the scar wide open and more blood spewed out. Larry was bleeding to death right on the spot. Peter left him there and headed for his squad car with Larry's alcohol-infused blood staining his uniform.

It wasn't until more than an hour later, when two customers stepped outside for a quick smoke, that Larry was discovered lying in a deep pool of his own blood with his eyes wide open and neck barely still attached to his body. Morbid curiosity ran through the bar with the speed of summer lighting and those inside who were not faint of heart stepped outside to gawk at the rigor mortis-bound carcass of one of the most foul characters ever to step inside The Belly Up.

Repeated 911 calls were made to the ambulance and to the police. The ambulance arrived in ten minutes.

No one could quite figure out why the Chief of Police did not respond to the 911 calls.

No one but Lou, that is.

Chapter Thirty-Six

Muldoon's cell phone was ringing but neither he nor Helenka heard it the first three times Lou dialed the number. Both of them had fallen asleep while watching "Harvey". The day had been too long and there had been too much wine drunk and warm flames from the hearth created the perfect atmosphere for both of them to doze off. What they were dreaming about what anybody's guess.

But it was Mugsy's bark that woke Muldoon. He had an inbred ability to awake suddenly when prompted by unfamiliar noises – and Mugsy almost never barked. When he did, Muldoon snapped to attention and realized that it was nearly two o'clock in the morning. The beautiful Helenka was fast asleep on his couch and his cell phone was ringing in the kitchen. He went in to silence it before it brought Helenka to a wakened state. He was about to mute the ringer when he noticed that it was Lou calling.

"Do you have any idea what time it is?" he asked Lou.

"Never mind what time it is" said Lou excitedly "where have you been? I've been ringing your cell phone for over an hour!!"

"I was asleep on the couch" he replied, volunteering no more information than that "why have you been calling me for an hour, anyway?"

"There's been a murder at The Belly Up!!" shouted Lou

Muldoon listened in disbelief. "What?"

"You heard me! Larry Lutursky had his throat cut out in the parking lot in back of the bar. And he had his face slashed, too. There were pools of blood everywhere. Two guys coming out for a smoke found him lying in the corner at about one o'clock......it was a grizzly sight!!"

"Are you at The Belly Up now?"

"Yes" was Lou's reply "been here since about 9:30 or 10 pm."

"Was Larry in the bar?"

"Not since I came in....but listen to this, Muldoon. People were calling 911 frantically....to both the hospital and the police."

"What did Branderford do?"

"Nothing...not a thing." said Lou "'cause he never showed up!"

There was an artic chill that ran through Muldoon like none he ever felt before – not even in the worst of circumstances when he was on the force in the big city.

"Never?"

"Nope....the ambulance carted Larry off in a body bag...probably to the morgue... but Branderford never responded. Nobody could understand why he was AWOL on this call, but let me tell you....I took one look at Larry's neck and I knew. It was practically severed from his body. I'll tell you what I think..."

Muldoon interrupted him "No need.....my immediate suspicion is probably the same as yours."

"Too right" said Lou "I think Branderford is out there somewhere with Larry's blood all over him"

"What's going on at the bar right now?'

"Well.....Eric took over the bar at midnight and after the ambulance left he locked the back door and told everybody to stay out of the parking lot until the police arrived. Nobody's car was parked out there anyway so it's just Larry's blood out there drying up."

"Is the bar still crowded?'

"Not really.....lots of people left after they heard about the murder....there's only a few still left here but Eric has to stay open until 4am anyway."

"Get out of there." Muldoon said

"What?"

"Get out of there and go home. Don't go back to the bar until you hear from me...do you understand?"

"But, what if..."

Again Muldoon cut him short. "Did you hear me?! I said get out of there and go home!"

Lou agreed and Muldoon hung up.

He set the cell phone down on the counter and turned the power off. He did not want to hear from anyone right now. He had to think. There was no doubt in his mind who murdered Larry. The only question remaining was where the murderer might be right now.

"You went too far again, Peter" Muldoon whispered "You lost your cool again and went beyond the bend this time. But, where's that bend going to take you, I wonder?"

He walked quietly into the living room and tapped Helenka softly on the shoulder until her eyes began to open. She sat up and tried to look at her watch.

"It's two o'clock in the morning." he said helping her out "we must have fallen asleep watching the movie."

She blinked her eyes a few times and pulled her hair back "2 am!!" she said "I should have been home hours ago!"

"I know" he said apologetically "I'm sorry.....I fell asleep, too. We can always blame it on the baklava!"

Helenka looked at the two empty plates where the desert used to be "Say nothing of the wine." she added

"Why don't you camp out upstairs until daylight? I can stay down here until you're ready to go home. You'll find everything you need in the bathroom and it's a comfy bed."

"I'm sort of ready to go home now."

"Helenka....it's 2:00 am...it doesn't make any sense to drive you home at this hour. You'll be safe upstairs....don't worry.....I'll send Mugsy up with you to guard you!"

"Mugsy is going to guard me against you?" she teased "Your own dog?"

"Go on Miss Patti-cake......there's a light at the top of the stairs."

She got up and turned towards the stairs but not before smacking him on the butt "It's Helenka....."

Muldoon feigned injury and laughed as he fell prostrate on the couch. He took a pillow and propped it under his head and dragged the couch blanket over him. "Oh yeah....that's right....I forgot" he said with a smile "Mugsy...take the lady Helenka upstairs, will you? Guard her with your life!"

Halfway up the stairs, Mugsy started to growl and began to bark again.

"Mugsy...I said guard her with your life....don't eat her up!"

Helenka stepped back a few stairs until she could see out the front window at what might be bothering Mugsy.

She ran down the rest of the stairs over to the couch. "Muldoon!!! There's a police car coming up your drive with no lights on!"

Muldoon lept from the couch to the front door in two steps and peered out. It was Peter. He was in the squad car. No lights on. Creeping forward at no more than five miles an hour.

"Get upstairs! Now!" he ordered "Take the dog with you!"

"No!! I'm not going up there.....what's going on here? Is that Branderford in that car....what's he doing out here in the middle of the night?! I told you he was dangerous!"

Muldoon did not answer her. He moved quickly over to the drawer underneath the dvd cabinet and pulled out his gun….a .45 automatic… checked the clip and took the safety off.

"Jesus, Muldoon!!" cried Helenka "what are you doing?"

If you don't get upstairs now, you will be laying on this couch where I plant you!"

She took a seat on the couch and drew Mugsy near. "What are you doing?" she asked again

"Shhhhhhh…" he said "don't say a word and don't move."

Peter stopped his car about twenty yards from the cabin's front porch. Muldoon watched him step out of the driver's seat and could see, even if only by the light of the moon, that he was covered in blood.

"Muldoon Frickey!!!! Muldoon Frickey….are you in there? You are under arrest!" Peter shouted. He fired a warning shot into the air.

Muldoon reached over and turned on the front porch flood-light. Peter flinched and opened up his car door to stand behind it. It was clear now to Muldoon that he was using the car door for support. The floodlight revealed the real condition of his uniform and it was utterly soaked in blood. His face had the look of a madman.

"Don't make me come in there, Muldoon!" was Peter's flacid warning as he fired another warning shot into the air. "Why did you have to come up here and ruin everything for me?"

"Don't do anything stupid, Peter" Muldoon shouted back "You know full well what a good shot I am! Just put your gun down and be done with it. If I fire, I will drop you….you know that! Just put your gun down now and call it a night!"

With not much aim, Peter fired three shots into the cabin breaking nothing more than glass windows.

"I'm warning you, Peter….next time I will fire back. Lay down your gun!"

Peter fired again right through the broken glass in the window. It missed Muldoon by a hair, hit the window frame and ricocheted right past Mugsy's left hind quarter – grazing him as it whizzed by. He let out a yelp as he fell forward into Helenka's lap.

Muldoon whipped around to see what happened and saw the look on Helenka's face.

He aimed his .45 out the window frame with Peter in his sights.

BAM!! BAM!! Two shots directly into his chest. Peter Branderford, the corrupt cop, dropped like a brick. Dead as a stone.

He jumped over to the couch and asked Helenka if she was alright. All she could do was nod. She was speechless and still holding Mugsy's head in her lap. Muldoon darted into the kitchen for his cell phone. He had Doc's number on speed dial and he hit the button.

He darted back into the living room and gave the phone to Helenka "I just called Doc Carlin….when he answers, tell him we are on our way in town to his office with Mugsy."

Muldoon lifted the dog mattress from its spot near the hearth and ran outside to throw it in the back of his truck never once even glancing at Peter. Muldoon knew he was dead. He was just *that* good of a shot.

He crouched down near Helenka and started to lift Mugsy up. Aside from a few whimpers, Mugsy was quiet. Muldoon could tell that it was just a scratch but his dog was bleeding. He laid him on the mattress in the back of the truck and motioned for Helenka to jump up.

He picked up a blanket from the truck bed and gave it to her. "Just compress this over his wound …..not too much pressure…..

just enough to soak up the bleeding…we'll be at Doc's in less than ten minutes."

Helenka stared at Mugsy and then up at Muldoon. She finally spoke. "What about him?" motioning her head over to Peter's body.

"Him?" said Muldoon "that prick just shot my dog. Let him lay there. He's dead anyway."

He hopped off the bed and into the driver's seat and barreled out of the driveway towards town pushing his truck to seventy miles an hour.

Peter Branderford was history. As were Wanda Skudnick and her son, Paul….Esperanza….Wally and even the contemptible Larry Lutursky. All dead.

It was all over now.

Epilogue

Before the week was out, Nick Spalata was officially re-installed as the town's Chief of Police. He graciously came out of his forced retirement out on the far end of Frettyman Lake .

A brief coroner's inquest found no suspicious circumstances surrounding Peter's death. All agreed that Muldoon acted in self-defense.

When contacted about her former husband's death, Jennifer Branderford ordered that his body be cremated and the remains disposed of. She wanted nothing to do with his personal effects. So, what was not thrown out by volunteers from the Chamber of Commerce was collected by the Salvation Army.

Larry Lutursky got buried in the section of Saint Maire Anthony's cemetery known as "potter's field" - a place to bury the indigent. It was next to the section for burial of the unknowns. So, it was pauper's graves for both Larry and Wally.

Mugsy was treated like royalty when Muldoon got him back home. The Irish Wolfhound snapped back to his old self in a matter of days and was running around the back yard in a week. "You're a tough 'ol hound…..I told you that when I first brought you home from the pound." Muldoon kept telling him. "I'll bet you just can't wait 'till we get our next case, can you…you 'ol ruffian!" With those words, Mugsy ran around the other side of the cabin from Muldoon, who would flop into the deck lounge in hysterics and yell out to him "C'mon 'ol boy…c'mon back here…..can't we at least talk about it!!"

Muldoon phoned Helenka and asked her out on a proper date….at a proper restaurant…..with a proper desert cart.

Meanwhile….back at The Belly Up, Pietro hung huge signs in both the Ladies' *and* Men's bathrooms that clearly said "No Drugs=No Drama" and Carl was still pestering customers for the name of their favorite actress while Johnny Cash songs filled the air of the old bar. Things had returned to normal and it was business as usual.

And…Yevgrev Andreovitch was rumored to have returned to Russia -- for now.

THE END